Balloon
Race
Mystery
and other stories

Joan Weir

OVERLEA
HOUSE

Published by: Overlea House
                20 Torbay Road
                Markham, Ontario
                Canada L3R 1G6

Cover art: Pamela Davies

R.L.: 4-6

Canadian Cataloguing in Publication Data

Weir, Joan Sherman, 1928–
   Balloon race mystery and other stories

ISBN 0-7172-2395-7 (bound)   ISBN 0-7172-2396-5 (pbk.)

I. Title.

PS8595.E48B35 1988   jC813'.54   C88-094611-3
PZ7.W44Ba 1988

123456789   WC   7654321098

Printed and Bound in Canada.

For Ian, Paul, Michael and Rich—
Mystery Club supporters
from the very beginning
—with love.

CONTENTS

Field Trip Folly

Wednesdays were special at Canville Elementary School.

Not because there were always hotdogs for lunch on Wednesdays, and not because once Wednesday arrived it meant that another school week was almost half over. Wednesdays were special because that was the day the Canville Elementary School Mystery Club met in the school library.

It had taken just about all the ingenuity Mike Adair and Tony Rossi possessed to get the club started. Mystery clubs, it seemed, didn't rank all that high on their school principal's list of priorities. But that was before Mr. Tate attended one of their meetings. Now, he was actually enthusiastic about the club.

"So why are you so glum all of sudden?" Tony Rossi asked, turning to the boy walking beside him. It was a sunny January morning, the first day of classes after the Christmas holidays.

A sheepish grin came over Mike Adair's face. "Admission of defeat."

Tony stopped walking and stared at his friend in amazement. "If you're admitting defeat, I'm Michael Jackson," he said in a now-I've-heard-everything tone of voice.

"I hope you've got a good singing teacher lined up, because I'm serious," Mike told him. He shoved his hands deeper into the pockets of the ski jacket he'd received for Christmas. "Why didn't I keep my big mouth shut for a change?"

Tony answered in a mock serious voice, "That is the question I've asked myself every one of the eighty-seven times you've managed to talk us into a detention. But school has just started this term, so how can you be in hot water already?"

As Tony talked, Mike took his hands out of his pockets and idly scooped up a handful of fresh snow. He shaped it into a ball, then his casual pose suddenly disappeared. "Catch!" he called, as the snowball came hurtling toward Tony's exposed neck.

With surprising swiftness, Tony's hand flashed up. The snowball nestled safely into his mittened palm.

Mike's eyes gleamed approval. "Have the

Blue Jays heard about you?''

''Yeah, but I told 'em they'd have to wait.'' Tony sounded bored. ''A guy's never going to make his mark in the world if he quits school before he graduates from fifth grade.''

Mike's grin widened. But the next moment he was looking glum again.

''So what's this about?'' Tony said quietly, realizing Mike wasn't going to tell him what was the matter unless he asked.

Mike gave his friend a grateful glance. ''The Mystery Club.''

''What's to worry? Everything's going great. Sure, last term things were iffy. We were always worried Mr. Tate might close us down. But this term he's actually encouraging people from less popular clubs to come and join us.''

Mike's hands went back into his pockets. ''That's the problem. Mr. Tate's chief argument for getting them to join was a promise that the first two mysteries in January would be specially planned for them—one tied in with stamp collecting and the other with hiking. The problem is that now we've got to deliver.''

''You said before Christmas that you had something already made up for the hiking people.''

Mike pushed impatiently at the thick shock of brown hair that, as usual, was falling over his forehead. "That was before Christmas. I looked at it again yesterday and it's awful. Which is why I should have kept my big mouth shut. If I hadn't said anything one of you other people might have come up with something over the holidays. Now there's no time."

"Can't you fix it?"

"Only one thing will fix it, and that's burial."

Tony's freckled face regained its look of unconcern. "I still say what's to worry? Postpone the hikers' mystery till next week so you'll have time to fix yours up, then get somebody else to do a stamp mystery this week. After all, Mr. Tate didn't say which story had to be first."

For a moment Mike continued to scowl, then his expression changed. The hint of a gleam came into his dark eyes. "Yeah! That's exactly what we'll do. We'll postpone the hikers' mystery and get somebody else to do a stamp mystery this Wednesday."

Tony grinned smugly.

"We'll get *you* to do it."

Tony stopped grinning.

"Actually, it's your turn," Mike went on, warming to his subject. "I presented that last mystery before Christmas, remember?''

Tony knew from experience how hard it was to try to change Mike's mind once it was made up, but Goliath had been pretty set in his ways until David had tackled him. With that thought, Tony straightened his shoulders and set his jaw. "No way. All I know about stamps is that they're something people never seem to have when they need them, and that if you lick too many you feel sick."

He paused. The very fact that this Goliath hadn't interrupted was encouraging. Taking two quick steps, Tony kicked at the soft snow on the edge of the sidewalk, raising a glistening curtain of white. "Why don't you ask Laura?" he suggested.

"About getting sick?"

"About a mystery. She's a stamp buff."

For the first time on the entire walk to school Mike's face looked hopeful. As soon as they arrived at the school entrance, he left Tony and went in search of Laura Gower.

"Actually, I've been working on an idea," Laura admitted when Mike explained what he wanted her to do.

"Can you have it ready in time for Wednesday?"

Laura's usually sunny expression changed to one of shock. "There's no way I can have it ready that soon. But I'll have it for next week. Okay?"

Mike had to be satisfied. He knew coaxing would be a waste of time. If there was any possible way that Laura could have had her mystery ready earlier she'd have said so.

He dumped his new ski jacket in his locker, collected his books, and went in search of Tony.

He located him easily in the crowded corridor outside the grade five classroom. Tony's carrot-red hair stood out against the background of brown and black heads around him.

"It's back to square one for this week's Mystery Club meeting," he announced, and he explained about Laura. "So what'll we do?"

Before Tony could answer, the bell rang.

It was recess before Mike had a chance to speak to Tony again. Mr. Proctor, their grade five homeroom teacher, had deliberately separated them so that their desks were on opposite sides of the room.

"How are we going to come up with a hikers' mystery in only two days?" Mike moaned, joining Tony in the hallway and picking up the discussion where they'd left off before class.

They collected their jackets from their lockers and headed for the playground. "The one you've been working on really won't do?'' Tony asked.

Mike shook his head firmly.

For a moment they walked in silence. Then with a smile, Tony pulled off one mitt and raised his hand to an invisible hat, one finger extended.

It was the signal they used on the completion of one of their Secret Emergency Plans. But instead of returning the gesture, Mike just scowled. "What have Secret Emergency Plans got to do with hikers?" he grumbled.

"Maybe lots. At least it's worth a try. After all, it was a SEP that kept Windy Jackson from quitting in December and bringing the whole Mystery Club crashing down around our ears."

Mike's eyebrows raised a fraction as he thought over what Tony had said. Then, unbuttoning the top pocket on his multi-pocketed safari pants, he pulled out their handwritten list of Secret Emergency Plans, with "Not to be shown to anybody" written underneath the title.

It contained six plans listed by number:

> #1. Ingenuity,
> #2. Persistence,
> #3. Surprise,
> #4. Diversion,
> #5. Confusion,

#6. Flattery.

As Mike glanced down the list thoughtfully, the frown returned. "I dunno," he said. "SEP #1 is no good because ingenuity seems to be something we're out of at the moment. SEP #2 is no better, because we've got to have time to be persistent. How about SEP #3?"

Tony thought for a moment, then shook his head.

"Diversion, then?"

Again Tony shook his head.

By this time Mike was looking as depressed as he had been earlier. Then suddenly his face lit up. "Hey! SEP #5! Maybe that would work!" And lowering his voice so no one else in the playground could hear, he explained to Tony what he was thinking.

Tony nodded happily. "I'm sure Laura will help," he said.

Two days later the Mystery Club assembled for its first meeting after the Christmas holidays. All the regular members were present, with eleven new faces—six from the now defunct Stamp Club and five from the Hiking Club.

"Our mystery is going to be a bit different this time," Mike explained as soon as the room was quiet. "Instead of one person telling the story, three of us are going to, and you've got to decide which story is the true one. Okay?''

He paused briefly, then began, "I belong to a neighbourhood Outdoor Club."

"For real?" Windy Jackson asked quickly. Windy was tall and thin with an overly long butch cut that gave his face a startled expression. "Do the kids in your neighbour-hood have a Nature Club too?"

Tony nudged him sharply in the ribs. "Smarten up, okay? It's a made-up story."

Windy slouched in his chair, but not before muttering in a disgusted tone that carried to everyone in the room, "I didn't figure the guys on your street were into neat things like nature clubs."

"As I said, we have an Outdoor Club," Mike continued, "and last spring we decided to go on a weekend hike. There's a rustic camp with some log cabins at McQueen Lake where school classes sometimes go for Science study. It's about twenty kilometres due north of town and perfect for hiking trips because it's right in the middle of nowhere. It's surrounded by thick forests and mountains on three sides and has the lake on the fourth."

Mike glanced at the hikers. To his delight all five of them were listening intently.

"The one bad thing about the McQueen

Lake Camp is that there's only one road leading into it, and that crosses a rickety wooden bridge over the McQueen River.''

The hikers exchanged glances.

"We picked a weekend late in February for our camp out," Mike went on, "because we figured that by February the weather was sure to be fairly mild. But January and February recorded the heaviest snowfall and the coldest temperatures in twenty-five years! Three days before we were to head out we almost cancelled because of the cold. Then, thank goodness, it warmed up. It was unbelievable. The day before we left the temperature jumped from minus eighteen degrees Celsius to plus six, and by Saturday morning it had climbed to twelve. When we reached McQueen Lake Camp at four o'clock that afternoon, we were hiking in our shirt sleeves.

"The following day was just as beautiful. The sky was cloudless and there wasn't a trace of wind. It was so nice we decided to take one final hike up the mountain slope behind the camp to look at the view before we headed home.

"The sun was so warm we hated to leave, but by half past three we figured we'd better. Not because it would be dark before we got home—that didn't worry us since we knew we'd be following a clearly-marked road—but we didn't want our folks to start worrying. So we came down from the mountain, packed up our gear and headed off.

"But,"—Mike's voice dropped dramatically—"when we reached the McQueen River we realized we were in trouble. We'd been hearing this strange whooshing noise for quite a while, only we hadn't paid attention to it. Now we found out what it meant. While we'd been basking in the sunshine, the warm weather had been melting the record snowfall on the mountainsides. The river had swollen to three times its usual size, and the rickety wooden bridge we'd crossed the day before was nowhere to be seen. The rushing torrent of water had swept it away."

Again Mike glanced at the hikers. They were watching him intently. "We knew there was nothing to do but try to find some other way across the river," he went on. "We headed off, but it was starting to get dark. Following a well-marked road in the dark was one thing, but making our way through thick forests in country we didn't know was quite another. Within half an hour we were completely lost."

"I bet you were scared," Sven said, getting into the spirit of the story.

Mike nodded. "I'll say. We knew the only thing to do was make camp for the night and wait for daylight to find our way home. The rising sun would tell us where east was and we'd know which way to walk.

"Only," added Mike ominously, "overnight the temperature dropped sharply. By morning a blanket of fog hung right down to ground level. We couldn't see more than ten metres in any direction, and it was impossible to tell where the sun actually was."

"What did you do?" Angie Thompson asked. She was one of the hikers, a tall, athletic-looking girl wearing black cords and a blue-jean jacket.

"We were pretty scared," Mike admitted. "At first we didn't know what to do. Then I remembered that there was another way to tell direction. Leaving the others at the campsite, I headed into the woods. It took a little while to find exactly what I needed, but at last I spotted an area where the trees weren't too thickly grouped, where on a clear day lots of sun could get between them. I checked them carefully, one at a time. Then I went back to where the others were waiting. 'This way,' I called.

"Of course, that started the jokes flying. 'I suppose the tree fairies gave you directions,' somebody quipped. 'Are you counting on the birds to direct us?' said another. But I ignored them. I insisted that everybody had to walk in the direction I said, and sure enough, within a couple of hours we were back in country we recognized. We found the river and followed it for an hour or so until we came to an old footbridge that was so high above the water it hadn't been damaged by the flood. We crossed that and, still using the trees for guidance, kept going till we found a road. After that it was easy.''

All at once Tony was on his feet. "Except it wasn't you who got us out of trouble,'' he objected in a loud voice. "I was the one who came up with the idea that saved us. I'd brought my black lab retriever along. In spite of your objections, I might add. And she's what saved us. When we saw that the bridge had been washed away I told Spooky to 'Go home'. Right away she obeyed. We followed, and she led us right home.''

There was a rustle of movement as the members of the audience exchanged glances. Then Laura got to her feet. "It's just like you boys to hog the limelight,'' she said sarcastically, "but I'm afraid you both have pretty short memories. I agree you told your dog to go home, Tony. But if you remember, she headed straight for the river bank where the bridge had been washed away. Then she jumped in, and without a thought for the rest of us, swam across and headed for the comfort of her nice warm doghouse. I can still see you jumping up and down on the river bank yelling at her. She didn't even stop to listen.''

Delighted giggles came from the listeners.

"And Mike's story is almost as bad. It's true, he was the one who said we should make camp for the night after we got lost, and he was also the one who came up with the idea of using the morning sun as a direction fix. But when the thick fog made that impossible, he was stymied. He didn't come up with any crazy plan that used the trees for direction. He just sat there and waited till I came up with the idea that saved us—which was to make flares.''

A rustle of movement greeted this remark as people exchanged glances.

"I broke some branches off the trees," Laura went on, "and tied on wads of paper torn from the notebooks we'd brought along with us. Then I looked for some clear spots where I could plant the flares in the ground and set them alight. Sure enough they attracted the attention of the forest rangers in a look-out station.

"I admit it took a while before the rangers rescued us, because their station was at the very top of the mountain and at least fifteen kilometres away. It was hard to keep everyone from panicking because it was eerie just sitting there waiting in the thick fog. But I got them singing songs to help pass the time, and sure enough after about an hour the forest rangers arrived to rescue us.''

As Laura finished Mike turned to the audience. "That's the mystery," he said. "Which of these stories is the true one, and why wouldn't you believe the other two?''

There was a murmur of whispered conversation for a moment, then Angie raised her hand.

What was Angie's answer? Turn to page 145 and see if you are right.

Inventions for Sale

The following Wednesday when the members of the Mystery Club assembled in the school library together with six potential new members from the old Stamp Club, Laura had her mystery ready.

Dressed in jeans and the pink designer Polo shirt she'd received for Christmas, she moved to the front of the room. She set her notes on the lectern, because it was a club rule that members had to read their stories so that no important details would be accidentally omitted.

"My story is about a twelve-year-old Canadian inventor named Emannuel Morganstein," Laura began. "Manny lives in Vancouver, but he has gone to New York accompanied by his dad to market his newest inventions."

"Can't he market them in Canada?" Tony Rossi asked.

Laura scowled. "Just listen to the story. It will answer your question."

"What are the inventions?" Windy Jackson asked sharply from one end of the room's only chesterfield. Even sitting against the cushions he seemed to tower over the people around him.

"The first is a special anti-gravity device that attaches to the sprocket wheels of bicycles," Laura explained. "Once the rider gets his bike rolling he just kicks in this device and relaxes. Manny's invention keeps the pedals turning all by themselves."

"Boy, could I ever do with one of those on my paper route!" Tony exclaimed from his chair near the front.

"Manny's second invention is even better," Laura went on. "It's a set of special child-size remote-control television glasses. They look exactly like those sleep shields that movie stars wear. Manny designed them that way on purpose so that any moms or dads looking in on their kids will think they're asleep. But hidden inside the sleep shield is a miniature TV screen and a microphone to carry the sound track of whatever program is keyed in. No more arguing with parents about going to bed before a TV show is finished. Just climb into bed with a pair of Manny's TV glasses."

"You take the gravity device, I'll take the TV glasses," Mike Adair told Tony.

"I think I've changed my mind," Tony countered.

Windy was looking thoroughly disgusted. "Come on, you nerds. Those zany inventions aren't real." His chin had lifted and his butch cut seemed to be standing at attention. "Are they part of the mystery?" he asked turning back to Laura.

"Not directly, but they're the reason Manny and his dad are in New York. Somehow they have to sell Manny's inventions."

"Why?" It was Kathy Chiu who spoke this time. She was sitting right in front of Laura, wearing a denim skirt and a white blouse.

"They need the money. Manny's little sister Anna has to have an operation. The government will help with the medical bills, but that's only part of the total cost. London is the only place in Canada where the operation is performed right now, so Anna and her mom and dad have to fly there from Vancouver and stay for weeks or months till Anna is ready to go back home again. That's why Manny wants to sell his inventions, so his sister can have her operation and his parents can stop worrying about money."

"Does he sell them?" Tony put in.

Laura nodded. "There is this special international convention in New York where people with lots of money listen to presentations from people like Manny who have ideas to market. On the very first day of the convention a big French development company decides to buy both of Manny's inventions. They give him a cheque for $25 000, plus a contract to pay royalties on any sales that go over that amount.

"Manny and his dad are pretty happy. They leave the convention and go down to the lobby of the hotel to send a telegram to Vancouver. Manny's so excited that he actually pats the pocket of his jacket where the cheque is stashed."

"You must think we're pretty dumb, if you figure we'll buy that bit about invention-selling-conventions," Windy Jackson objected. He sounded even more disgusted.

"She'll think we're even dumber if we don't," Mike put in from across the room. He straightened the large number 99 on his T-shirt. "I saw a program about it on TV. There are conventions like that in lots of places—New York, Toronto, Europe, all over."

Laura ignored the interruption. "It's only mid afternoon when Manny sells his pedalling device and his TV glasses," she went on.

"His dad decides to go back to the convention for a while, but Manny wants to watch some *Star Trek* reruns that are scheduled on TV. He leaves his dad at the convention floor and goes up to the room.

"The TV programming in New York, however, is no more dependable than the TV programming in Canada. The *Star Trek* reruns have been pre-empted for a political speech by some election hopeful. Since Manny isn't interested in that, he decides to head over to Central Park. Next to making inventions and watching *Star Trek,* his favourite hobby is stamp collecting, and this particular weekend a special stamp collectors' display in the park has been advertised. He puts his jacket on and heads out of the hotel.

"It isn't till he's halfway to the park that he remembers about the cheque in his jacket pocket. He debates about taking it back to the hotel, but he hates to go all the way back. The stamp display might not be there too much longer because it's already after four o'clock. Besides, he tells himself, the cheque is probably safer in his pocket than in the hotel room. Nobody would ever suspect that a twelve-year-old boy was carrying a $25 000 cheque in his pocket.

"He's so busy thinking about what stamps

he should try to buy that he doesn't notice two men in raincoats following him.

"Though Manny doesn't realize it, the same two men were in the lobby of the hotel when he and his father sent the telegram to Vancouver. They heard the news about the money, and they saw Manny pat his pocket."

Laura paused for a moment to consult her notes. "By this time Manny has reached the stamp display booths at the park entrance. Now he's really excited, because he's never seen anything so fabulous. More than a dozen booths have been set up with stamps from all over the world. Not just everyday stamps, either. Some of them are so rare and valuable that Manny can't believe the price tags!"

"Five figures?" Mary-Lyn Goltz asked quickly. She was a small, dark-haired girl, one of the Stamp Club members.

"Even six in some cases," Laura replied.

"Does that mean he can't buy any?" Mary-Lyn went on in a voice that suggested she understood just how Manny would have felt.

Laura shook her head. "Fortunately they aren't all expensive. Manny finds some South African Boer War stamps which don't cost too much at all. He's just trying to decide which of them to buy when the men in raincoats move up on either side of him. 'What do you mean by running off like that?' they demand loudly to fool any listeners. 'Don't you realize how worried we've been?' And before Manny realizes what is happening, they take his arms and propel him out of the stamp booth. While he is still trying to collect his wits, they seize the cheque out of his jacket pocket, force him to sign it, and disappear into the park at a run.''

''Why doesn't he call for help?'' Sven Olafsen put in sharply.

''He does. But by the time the police finally come it's too late. The two men have disappeared.''

''Can't the police find them?''

''Eventually, but they have to search the whole park which takes almost an hour. And when the men are finally found they no longer have the cheque. In fact, they don't even look as if they're guilty. They are sitting innocently on a park bench eating ice cream cones.

''This makes the police wonder if Manny is making the story up. After all, twelve-year-old boys don't as a rule wander around Central Park with cheques for $25 000 in their pockets. But fortunately one of the police officers recognizes Manny. He's seen a news report on television about the convention, and Manny had been interviewed as the youngest inventor present. It's just possible Manny could be telling the truth. So to be on the safe side the police decide to take the two men to police headquarters until they have time to do more checking.

"As soon as they leave with the robbers, Manny starts searching the park. He searches everywhere. Then he goes back to the hotel and gets his dad and they search some more. They search in garbage bins, behind trees, and under bushes. They check under the tables in the stamp display booths, and under the hoods of the cars in the parking lot.

"Next morning, exhausted and discouraged, they go to the police station. Maybe the police will have discovered something, they tell themselves.

"The police officers shake their heads. 'For a moment we thought we might be in luck,' they admit. 'We found a secret pocket in the lining of one of the men's coats. But it was empty.'

" 'Completely empty?' Mr. Morganstein says.

" 'Except for an empty envelope.'

" 'Did you keep it?' Manny asks quickly. 'Maybe the address will give us a clue to where the cheque is hidden.'

"The police officer gives his partner a look

revealing what he thinks about the imagination of small boys. 'We kept it all right. It's with the rest of their things. But you can forget about any clue. It's just an old envelope. It's even got stamps on it—two of them—and one has a post office cancellation mark on it.'

"Manny is getting pretty desperate. The cheque has to be somewhere! The men couldn't have eaten it! As a last resort he asks if he can see everything that was in the men's pockets.

"Again the police exchange amused looks, but they humour him. They set everything out on a table: the empty envelope with its one cancelled stamp, a ring of keys, a folder of half-used matches, two filter-tip cigarettes in a pouch pack, three pieces of gum and a pocket journal.

"The minute the journal is set down on the table Mr. Morganstein picks it up. Eagerly he scans each entry. But there is nothing to give them any clue about the money.

"As Manny studies the objects he thinks back over his search of the park. He imagines each spot in turn. Suddenly his face brightens. 'It's all right!' he cries delightedly, reaching for one of the objects on the table. 'Anna can have her operation after all! The money is safe!' "

Laura looked up from her notes. "What object did Manny reach for, and what did he mean, the money was safe? Where was it?"

Three of the stamp club members had their hands waving almost before Laura finished speaking, but Mary-Lyn's was the first.

What was Mary-Lyn's answer? Turn to page 147 and see if you are right.

Brain Teasers

When the thirty-two students in Mr. Proctor's grade five class reassembled after recess the following morning, they expected to be studying Science, as they always did third period on Thursdays. Most of them were already getting their workbooks out of their desks when Mr. Proctor told them "We're going to do something a little different this morning."

The class looked with interest at the tall, greying homeroom teacher.

"Mr. Tate has asked me to pass along a message to those students in this class who are members of the Mystery Club," Mr. Proctor continued. "The other grade five teachers who also have students in the club will be doing the same."

The interested looks grew more pronounced. It wasn't often that school principals sent messages to grade fives.

"Because of the good reports Mr. Tate has received concerning the mysteries presented recently, and because of the interest expressed by a number of parents, Mr. Tate is considering having the club members present a mystery at the next Parents' Night."

An excited buzz of comments arose from the club members. Mr. Proctor ignored it. "I realize that only eight or nine of you here belong to the Mystery Club, but in light of Mr. Tate's plan I am going to use our Science class this morning to test everyone's quickness and powers of observation." He gazed over the rows of students.

Mike threw a come-on-guys-we've-got-to-measure-up look first at Tony, then at Laura, and finally at Kathy. If the rest of the class got the answers and the club members didn't, they were going to look pretty foolish.

"I should warn you that these tests may not be as simple as they seem," Mr. Proctor cautioned, picking up a folded sheet of paper from the top of his desk.

"The first is a number puzzle. You should be able to do it quickly. Ready? Start with 4. Multiply by 5. Divide the total by 1/2 and add 7. Write down the number you end up with."

He looked over the rows of concentrating faces, allowed a moment for them to finish, then said, "How many of you had 17 as your answer?"

Twenty-eight hands waved excitedly.

"Unfortunately you're wrong," Mr. Proctor informed them.

He allowed another moment for those twenty-eight to do some rethinking, then continued, "The next puzzle concerns a pig farmer. Most people think that pig farms are smelly and dirty. That's because they've never visited the pig farm owned by Wilbur T. Jagg. The only smell at Wilbur T. Jagg's pig farm is one of new-mown hay, and the pigs are spotless. In fact, they have a bath every morning.

"You see, Farmer Jagg has invented a 'pig wash.' It works the same way as a car wash, except that no soap is used and the water is lukewarm instead of icy. The pigs love it, because contrary to popular belief, pigs do not like to be dirty. They roll in the mud to keep their skin damp, but they would much prefer to roll in clean water. Farmer Jagg's pigs can hardly wait for daybreak each morning so they can line up and wait for their turn to step up onto the moving platform and be carried through the water jets." Mr. Proctor was having a little trouble keeping a serious expression on his face.

"The reason Farmer Jagg has gone to all

the trouble of inventing a pig wash is so everyone in the whole world will know how clever he is. Not because of the wash— anyone could have invented that—but because of the pigs. You see they are colour coded."

An exchange of surprised looks greeted this remark for no one had ever heard of colour-coded pigs.

"As you know," Mr. Proctor went on, "different breeds of pigs have been developed with specific colour combinations, but as a rule all the pigs in a certain litter will have the same combination of colours. They will be all brown and black, for example, or all white and pink, or all brown, tan and white. But not so in Farmer Jagg's pig yard. Out of a total of sixteen pigs, three are pink, but only one of the three is entirely pink. The second is pink with black spots, and the third is pink with a black tail. Seven other pigs are white, but two of the seven have black spots and another has a pink tail. One pig is completely brown. There are two brown and black pigs, and the remaining three pigs are black and white."

Mr. Proctor waited as everyone busily scribbled down figures. "As I mentioned a moment ago, Farmer Jagg is extremely proud of his colour-coded pigs. He travels all over the country bragging about them. Which brings me to my question.'' He glanced back at his sheet of notes for a second. ''How many of Farmer Jagg's sixteen pigs can honestly say that they are different in colour from any of the others?''

As Mr. Proctor stopped speaking Mike took a quick glance around the classroom. People were figuring frantically, and almost every face was creased in a frown. Tony, in fact, was chewing thoughtfully on the end of his pencil and positively scowling at the notes he'd made.

Mike struggled to hide his grin and returned his attention to Mr. Proctor.

''Now for my final question,'' Mr. Proctor said when everyone seemed to have finished puzzling over Farmer Jagg. ''I want you to tell me if you think there is something wrong with this story. It takes place at the turn of the century and concerns an English army officer who was stationed in China at the time of the Boxer Rebellion. By the time the uprising is over, he is exhausted both physically and mentally. He is sent back to England on leave, but the strain of what he has seen and endured is not easily forgotten. He can't stop thinking about it and agonizing over it. He even finds himself dreaming about it.

"One Sunday he goes to church. Lulled by a long sermon, he falls asleep. He dreams he is in China. In the dream he is captured by the enemy and sentenced to death.

"Just as the executioner's axe is descending to cut off his head, his wife notices that he is sleeping. Lightly she taps him on the side of the neck with her fan.

"To the sleeping man the touch of the fan is the executioner's axe. The shock is so great that he dies instantly without awakening.

"The wife is prostrate with grief and guilt, for she feels that his death was her fault."

Mr. Proctor paused and looked solemnly over the faces gazing back at him so intently. "If you think something is wrong with the story, write it down, then let's see how well you have scored on my three powers-of-observation tests."

Pencils scribbled furiously. Mr. Proctor waited till they were still, then asked for volunteers to give the answers. A dozen hands shot up, including Mike's, Laura's, Kathy's and Tony's. But the first hand raised belonged to a wiry girl wearing glasses who was seated near the back. Her name was Liz Steiger but everyone called her Whiz.

What were Whiz's answers? Turn to page 148 and see if you are right.

Olympic Intrigue

W hen the lunch bell rang and Mike and Tony emerged from the classroom into the hallway, Liz Steiger was waiting.

"Can I join the Mystery Club?" she blurted out in a self-conscious rush.

Mike's eyes met Tony's above her head. He knew his friend would be thinking exactly what he was—that Whiz Steiger never got involved in any extra-curricular activities unless they had something to do with computers or science.

The reason was simple. Two years ago her dad had set up a science workshop for her in their basement, and last fall the family had bought a PC with lots of software. Now every afternoon as soon as school was over, and on Saturdays and Sundays, Whiz was either performing science experiments or playing Space Raiders. Which was why it was puzzling that she would suddenly—

"Could I present the mystery at the next meeting?" Whiz added in an even more self-conscious voice.

Mike's worries evaporated. Who cared why Whiz was suddenly a mystery buff? "Can you ever!" he exclaimed, and he gave Tony an exultant grin over Whiz's head.

Whiz pushed at her glasses as if they were riding too low on her nose, and with a shy smile hurried away.

"Her mystery has got to have something to do with science," Tony predicted as they walked home that afternoon.

Mike shook his head. "Computers, I bet."

For the next five days they debated off and on about what the topic of their newest club member's mystery would be. They still hadn't reached an agreement when the Mystery Club assembled in the library the following Wednesday.

Whiz waited till everyone was seated, then moved toward the lectern.

"My mystery is about a cryptanalyst," she began in a small, nervous voice. As she spoke she smoothed the sides of her jeans with shaking fingers.

Windy Jackson was sprawled, feet extended, in the room's most comfortable armchair. "She means a codebreaker," he announced in a smug voice.

A tinge of pink crept into Whiz's pale cheeks. Again she pushed at her glasses, then shook her head. "A codebreaker just works with codes," she said apologetically. "A cryptanalyst can break any kind of secret message, which is what the person in my story can do."

For a minute Windy looked like a small child caught with his hand in the cookie jar. In an effort to save face he blustered, "These mysteries are supposed to be about things we can work out. Nobody is going to be able to solve a mystery about some weird crypto-somebody-or-other, and a complicated code."

Instead of looking more uncomfortable, Whiz smiled, as if the exchange had restored her self-confidence. "Codes aren't hard, they're easy. If they weren't, people would make too many mistakes. Don't forget they're intended to be used by ordinary people."

Laura Gower edged forward in her chair. "How come you know so much about them?" she asked Whiz.

"I have an uncle in Ottawa who is a cryptanalyst," Whiz admitted.

"Is your mystery a true story then?"

"No. I made it up. But I got the idea from things my uncle has told me. Before I start, do you want me to describe some different kinds of codes so you'll have an idea what to look for?''

"Yes!" a dozen voices chorused.

The last trace of Whiz's self-consciousness disappeared. "The simplest codes use one letter in place of another," she explained.

"How do you mean?" Laura asked.

"Make twenty-six spaces in a row and write the letters of the alphabet in the spaces," Whiz explained. "Then underneath make twenty-six more spaces and write the alphabet again, only start in a different spot. Julius Caesar invented this code and he started two spaces over like this:

A B C D E F G H I J K L M N O P Q R S T U V W X Y Z
C D E F G H I J K L M N O P Q R S T U V W X Y Z A B

Now A was C, B was D and so forth. His grandnephew Augustus started *his* second line in the second space instead, so A became B, and B became C, which was much easier to remember."

As Whiz had been talking Windy's boredom had completely disappeared. Instead of sprawling full length in the chair he was sitting upright, his eyes shining. "Then 'Meet me at ten,' would be 'Nffu nf bu ufo'?'' he put in suddenly.

The next moment his face turned fiery red as the whole room stared at him. But before anyone could say anything that would embarrass him even more, Whiz continued calmly, "Right. Except the time would probably be changed as well. Usually people do that when they use code—move the time along an hour and a half so anyone breaking the code and trying to interfere will be too late."

"Hey! Neat!" Tony exclaimed.

"Another way to write in code is to print the message backwards," Whiz went on. "Instead of writing HELP, write PLEH. But the code I like best is what my uncle calls a password code. It's like Julius Caesar's, only before you fill in the alphabet in the second row, you print a password."

A frown had appeared on Tony's face. "Can you give us an example?"

"If you give me a password."

"INSPECTOR," he suggested.

Whiz nodded. "Write down the alphabet as before, then underneath, starting directly under the A, write:

INSPECTORABDFGHJKLMQUVWXYZ."

Mike studied what he had written. "What happens if the word you want to use as a password has some letters repeated?" he asked.

"Leave the repeated letters out. Otherwise you'll have more than twenty-six in the second row and the code won't work. For example, if you wanted to use 'Wednesday' you'd have to drop one of the Es and one of the Ds, and the second line would read: WEDNSAYBCFGHIJKLMOPQRTUVXZ."

Suddenly Mike had an idea. "Can you use a two-word password?" he asked, deliberately trying to keep the excitement out of his voice so no one would guess what he was thinking.

A gleam of amusement came into Whiz's eyes, making it pretty obvious that she had guessed, but all she said was "Of course."

Tony must have guessed too, because he was grinning.

But Laura had scarely been listening to Mike's questions. She was sitting forward in her chair, gazing at Whiz. "That's what I'm going to be when I grow up," she announced. "A cryptanalyst."

"Now here is my mystery," Whiz said. "It takes place during the Winter Olympics in Calgary." She waited to give everyone time to shift mental gears, then continued, "Everyone who lives in Calgary is excited about the Games, but the person who is most excited is

Mary O'Riley, the daughter of the Superintendent of the Calgary RCMP. Months ahead of time Mary buys tickets for as many of the events as she can. Then she reads and studies everything she can find on the athletes who are expected to come. She talks her teachers into letting her do a special research project on the Olympics so that she'll be able to attend the Games every day. It will mean missing some school, but she promises to make up all the missed work as soon as the Games are over.

"Mary's dad isn't too pleased when he hears about it—at least not at first. But then he decides maybe it's a good thing Mary is going to be at the Games after all, because on the very day the competitions are scheduled to begin, the RCMP receive a warning that one of the competing athletes may be in danger. The message claims that an athlete will be kidnapped, only it doesn't say when the kidnapping is going to take place, or which athlete is to be seized."

Whiz looked over the rows of listeners. Every face was watching her intently. "Hundreds and hundreds of athletes are taking part in the Olympic Games," she continued. "There is no way the police can watch over every one of them. The best plan they can come up with on the spur of the moment is to have one of their secret agents pretend to be a member of Canada's ski team and move into the athletes' village along with the competitors. Their hope is that by living right with the athletes this secret agent might be able to find out if someone really is in danger, and if so who it is.''

Tony was scowling. "How can a person pretend to be on an Olympic ski team unless they can really ski?''

"Secret Agent Petros *can* ski,'' Whiz replied. "Of course, he's not Olympic calibre, but each ski team takes along an alternate in case one of the regular team members has to drop out. In most cases nothing happens to the regular members so the alternate doesn't have to perform. That's what Petros and the RCMP are counting on.''

"Petros—what a neat name,'' Kathy put in.

Tony was shaking his head. "The risk would be too great. One of the team members could get sick and then this secret agent would have to enter the men's giant slalom or something. If that happened, Canada would look pretty foolish.''

"Not half as foolish,'' Mike interrupted "as if the person Petros had to replace was Canada's top hope for the women's downhill.''

Whiz struggled to keep from laughing. ''Nevertheless, the RCMP decide the risk is worth it. They move Petros into the athletes' village with the rest of the competitors, but they figure it won't hurt to have an extra pair of eyes and ears watching and listening as well. Since Mary, the Superintendent's daughter, is going to be at the Games every day, they ask her to keep an eye out too.

''For the first few days no one seems to be in any kind of danger, and both Petros and Mary start wondering if the warning was a hoax. But then Petros begins noticing things, and eventually he discovers that there actually is a kidnapping planned. It's scheduled for suppertime on the final Friday evening of the Games when security measures may be starting to let down.

''Immediately, he tells the RCMP, but it doesn't help them much because he still doesn't know which one of the hundreds and hundreds of athletes is the target.

''As the final Friday evening approaches, Petros gets more and more frantic. Which athlete is in danger? He has to find out. But how?

''Two o'clock comes, three o'clock, four o'clock. Petros realizes that he has failed and he feels awful.

"So does Mary, because she considers she is equally to blame. She feels so terrible that for the first time since the Games started, she decides to go home before the events are over. She goes to the bus turnaround and joins the line-up for her bus back downtown."

Whiz's voice took on an ominous note. "But as she stands waiting for the bus, she overhears a conversation. A man and a woman are discussing the kidnapping. They must figure they are pretty safe because they aren't even talking in code.

"Mary is so excited she can hardly keep still. As soon as she hears the name of the athlete they are planning to kidnap, she pushes her way out of the line-up and heads for the nearest pay telephone. She knows there isn't time to get downtown and then tell the RCMP what she has discovered because it is already almost five o'clock.

"Unfortunately her sudden decision to drop out of the line-up has alerted the kidnappers. They follow her to the phone booth, and as she dials her number and prepares to tell the RCMP her news, they pull open the door and glare at her threateningly.

"Mary is scared, but not so scared she can't think clearly. After all, she's spent her whole life in an RCMP officer's household, and she isn't going to give in without a struggle. As she waits for someone to answer the phone, she studies the faces of the man and woman looking at her. It's obvious from their expressions that they aren't quite sure if she actually is a danger to them, and until they are sure they don't want to do anything that might give their plot away.

"Now Mary knows what she has to do. She has to get her message across while there is still time for the police to act on it, but at the same time she has to make it sound as if she is talking about something perfectly ordinary. She has to convince the two people outside the phone booth that she doesn't know anything at all about kidnap plots."

Whiz paused for breath and glanced along the rows of faces. Everyone seemed thoroughly interested.

"At last an officer at police headquarters answers the phone. Mary knows she can't ask to speak to her father. That would give away the fact that she is talking to RCMP headquarters. So in her most casual voice she gives her name to the officer on the other end of the phone, then says, 'Will you please tell Dad that I won't be able to have dinner with him this evening after all?'

"She knows the RCMP officer is going to be pretty confused by this, because she never leaves personal messages for her dad at the station. But before he can say anything she hurries on, 'Also, he wanted me to get him the hockey scores. Will you pass them along? Toronto 1, Philadelphia 5; Montreal 5, Calgary 4; Edmonton 1, Boston 4. And in the other games, Washington 3, Detroit 3; New York 2, Winnipeg 5; Quebec 4, Vancouver 0. Thank you very much.' And before the officer can say a word, Mary hangs up the phone.

"The kidnappers are thoroughly confused because it sounded like a pretty innocent conversation. While they're trying to decide what to do, Mary calmly walks out of the phone booth and heads back to the bus line-up.

"The RCMP officer is almost as confused as the kidnappers, but he knows better than to ignore Mary's call. It has been taped, as are all telephone conversations going in to police headquarters, so he takes the tape to the Superintendent. The Superintendent listens, then calls in his top cryptanalyst. It takes the cryptanalyst exactly ten seconds to understand Mary's message. Instantly secret police are dispatched to the Olympic village and the athlete in danger is quickly whisked away to safety."

Whiz glanced along the rows of interested

faces. "That's my mystery. What was Mary's message, and how did she send it?"

To everyone's amazement Windy's hand was the first one raised.

What was Windy's answer? Turn to page 149 and see if you are right.

The Disappearing Ornaments

It was all Mike could do to contain his impatience while the club members tidied the library, put the chairs back where they belonged, and started home.

As soon as he and Tony were safely out of earshot, he turned excitedly to his friend. "Let's add a code to our Secret Emergency Plans. Okay?"

Tony grinned. "I had an idea that was what you were thinking when you asked all those questions."

"Whiz did too," Mike admitted. "So what do you think?"

"A password code, no doubt," Tony said innocently.

A sheepish look crept over Mike's face. "Was I that obvious?"

Tony scooped up a handful of snow, firmed it into a ball and hurled it at the stop sign at the corner of the intersection. "Yes, but that's because I can read your mind. The rest of the kids won't twig. They aren't even sure you've got a mind.''

An arm shot toward Tony's head. He ducked, and the arm whizzed by with room to spare. Looking smug and pleased with himself, Tony continued sauntering along the snowy sidewalk.

Mike took off his mitts, foraged into the middle pocket on his pants, and brought out the sheet of paper on which their Secret Emergency Plans were listed. "You wouldn't by any chance be bluffing about this sudden ability of yours to read my thoughts? Might there be a possibility that you are just pretending?" And before Tony realized what he intended, Mike held out the list and a pencil. "If we're going to add a secret code to our Secret Emergency Plans we've got to put down exactly what that code is going to be. I'll think it and you write it, okay?"

The grin disappeared from Tony's lips. Since Mike was continuing to hold out the list he had no choice but to take it, though he did so with marked reluctance.

A smirk crept over Mike's face.

Tony read the list through. He read it through a second time. He licked the end of his pencil. Then, as if he'd run out of ways to stall, he methodically pencilled in at the end of the list: "#7. Mystification," and held out the sheet.

Mike shook his head. "Nice try, Einstein, but that's not a code. You said you knew what I was thinking, so prove it."

Again Tony licked the point of the pencil, then beside "#7. Mystification," he added, "Secret Code."

"Keep going," Mike prodded.

Tony looked pleased with himself. Grinning broadly, he wrote: "Password—'Mystery Club' with one Y dropped."

All trace of smugness disappeared from Mike's expression. He licked his finger and made an invisible chalk mark in the air. "Round one goes to you," he conceded. "But watch out, I'll get you next time." Then in a different tone, he asked, "So what d'you think? Is it a good idea?"

"Great," Tony answered. "We'll teach the code to everybody in the club then write notes back and forth to each other all through class. We'll be a cinch to make the *Guinness Book of World Records* for the greatest number of detentions ever amassed by any grade five class."

Mike grinned appreciatively. "Funny, funny. So okay, we'll just use the code in absolute emergencies. How's that?"

"Better."

"Shall we wait till the next club meeting to tell everybody?"

Before Tony could reply a small dark figure catapulted itself between them. It was Rahoul Gurvinder, a grade three who lived in the same block as Mike and Tony. As a rule Rahoul's eyes bubbled with mischief, but today his face was pulled into a worried frown. Obviously he'd been looking for them for some time. He seized Mike's arm as if it was a life raft tossed to a drowning man. "It's next Wednesday," Rahoul said. The words came out in a breathless rush. "But nobody's got one, so what're we gonna do?"

The question of a club code was obviously going to have to wait, Mike decided, exchanging an amused glance with Tony.

Lots of people might have wondered what the worried little grade three was talking about, but Mike and Tony understood perfectly. Last term the Mystery Club had experimented with a special "junior" meeting. The grade twos, threes and fours had been invited, and one of their group was responsible for presenting the mystery. It had been so successful that the club had decided to have another, and the date selected was the following Wednesday.

"Somebody must have an idea," Mike returned.

Rahoul shook his head, his dark eyes worried.

"Not even DeeDee Wilkes?" Tony offered. He tried not to smile. He knew how Rahoul felt about DeeDee.

A look of disgust came over Rahoul's dark face. "Her stories are no good."

"What about Jamie Phillips?"

Again Rahoul shook his head.

"Then it's up to you," Mike stated firmly.

"But I don't know any—"

"Yes, you do. What about that story you told me—" And he bent down and whispered something in Rahoul's ear.

The boy's face broke into a smile. The next moment he was running happily back across the playground.

The following Wednesday the Mystery Club assembled for its second junior meeting.

"Actually, my mystery is a true story," Rahoul began in a breathless voice to the large group assembled in the library. "It happened a few weeks ago, just before Christmas."

He gazed excitedly along the rows of listeners. His eyes found Mike and he waited for a nod of encouragement. Then he took a deep breath and hurried on. "Most years we wait till just a few days before Christmas to put up our Christmas tree, but this year we put it up a whole week and a half early. We had to, because my dad had to be away on a business trip from December 16 till December 23, and my mom was going with him. They figured they'd be busy enough with last minute things after they got back without having to worry about the tree as well. So we put it up the night before they left.''

"I bet they didn't really let you help," DeeDee interrupted in a loud voice. "I always get to help put our tree up, but that's because girls are more de . . . deepen . . . dependentendable than boys." She struggled with the word.

"Dependable," Rahoul corrected angrily. "And they do so let me help. They even let my little sister help."

DeeDee smirked. "Your little sister doesn't even go to school yet."

"That doesn't mean she can't help decorate the Christmas tree," Rahoul insisted.

"Cut out the arguing," Windy Jackson snapped. He was fed up. He hadn't been all that crazy about the idea of allowing juniors to come to meetings in the first place, and this kind of wrangling convinced him he'd been right. "Either get on with the mystery or let the rest of us get out of here. Okay?"

DeeDee's face paled. She looked as though

she wished she could become invisible. She was scared of Windy.

Even Rahoul's voice quavered. "As I said, we put the tree up early," he went on. "The next day my mom and dad left on their trip, and the day after that, things started to disappear."

"How d'you mean, things started to disappear?" Jamie Phillips asked.

Some of the Mystery Club members had been on the point of asking the same thing, but they'd held back because this was supposed to be a mystery for only the junior visitors to solve.

"The things off the tree," Rahoul explained. "First the coloured ornaments, then the tinsel, and finally even a couple of small presents that my mom had wrapped all in shiny gold paper and put on one of the low branches."

"You mean somebody took them?" Jamie asked again.

Rahoul nodded. It was obvious that he was enjoying himself. "I was afraid my mom and dad would think it was me, 'cause the only other people in the house were my little sister and the baby-sitter. And that's when I went to get Mike to help."

There was a rustle of movement as two dozen bodies shifted in their chairs in an effort to locate Mike. He wriggled self-consciously. He'd asked to be left out of this, but obviously the only way Rahoul could tell his story was exactly the way it had happened.

"Mike said I shouldn't press the panic button," Rahoul went on. "He said if I hadn't taken the things off the tree, then we'd just have to work out who had."

"If it had happened to me," DeeDee interrupted in a boastful tone, "*I* wouldn't have needed to get help." She accented the pronoun. "*I*'d have worked it out myself. Obviously the person who took the things off the tree was your little sister."

"It was not!" Rahoul retorted. "She couldn't have reached. She's only this high." He held his hand out just above his waist.

"With that personality," Mike said under his breath to Tony, "I wonder what DeeDee is going to be when she grows up."

"Murdered," Tony whispered back.

"My sister couldn't have reached the ornaments that had been taken off way up high," Rahoul went on. "The only person who could have reached that high was the baby-sitter. Only why would she want to take Christmas ornaments?"

"Maybe somebody broke into the house while you were at school?" Jamie Phillips suggested.

Rahoul nodded slowly. "I thought of that. Only why would they have stolen ornaments off the tree that weren't worth anything and left the really valuable things in the house like the stereo and VCR?"

DeeDee Wilkes was still not finished. "I bet they hadn't been taken at all," she said in a superior tone. "I bet they'd just fallen off. If I'd been there I'd have looked all around the bottom of the tree, under the furniture and everything, and I bet—"

"Then you'd have lost," Rahoul cut her off sharply. "Because I looked before I went to ask Mike for help, and they weren't there."

Mike exchanged a glance with Tony. He knew what Tony was thinking: that DeeDee could very easily have been right. It wouldn't have been surprising if the ornaments had been knocked off the Christmas tree at Rahoul's house because everybody in the whole school knew that the place was just one step away from being an animal sanctuary. Rahoul was always talking about it. His family had two big dogs, and a cat that had just presented them with three baby kittens. Mrs. Gurvinder had made a pet of a black and white magpie that lived in a nest in the big poplar tree just outside the kitchen window. Rahoul's sister had a pet canary and Rahoul had two pet gerbils.

All the animals roamed freely in the house whenever they liked. To make it easy for the cats and the dogs to come in from the fenced back yard, Mr. Gurvinder had put a hinged panel in the kitchen door. The bird could come in whenever it wanted to because winter and summer Mrs. Gurvinder left the kitchen window open. She also left birdseed and oatmeal on the kitchen counter. As a result the bird didn't even fly south during the cold weather anymore.

Rahoul's sister's pet canary was almost as bad. It was allowed to fly free in the house too. And even the gerbils ran free in the living room every evening when Rahoul played with them. With all those creatures running and climbing and flying around, it wouldn't have surprised anyone if all the ornaments had been knocked off sooner or later.

"But the ornaments were nowhere in the house," Rahoul insisted. "Mike came back with me and we looked and looked.

"By this time I was feeling pretty awful. In just a few more days my mom and dad would be home, and I was afraid if they found all those things missing they'd think I'd been playing a trick on them or something. But just as I was sure I was in awful trouble, Mike came up with the answer."

He glanced briefly at Mike to see if he'd missed anything, then finished, "Where were the ornaments and who had stolen them?"

The regular members of the Mystery Club were all grinning delightedly, but they knew they weren't to answer so they waited. At last Jamie Phillips raised his hand. "I know," he said.

What was Jamie's answer? Turn to page 151 and see if you are right.

Four Minute Wonder

The news that Mr. Tate intended to ask the Mystery Club members to present a mystery at the next Parents' Night spread through the school. The following afternoon when Butch Ogrodnick and Tim Silverstein spotted Sammy Jack crossing the playground, it was too good an opportunity to miss.

Butch and Tim were in Mr. Carlysle's grade five class. Two against one on Sammy was always one of their favourite pastimes, but now it promised to be particularly entertaining since they had something concrete to bug him about. Cutting diagonally across the field, they blocked his progress.

"Are you guys really gonna make everybody's parents sit through one of your Mystery Club drags?" Butch asked in a sarcastic voice as soon as they were close enough. "Do you hate adults that much?" And he launched into a rifle-quick loud-voiced attack that caught poor Sammy completely off guard. Even if he'd been able to think of a reply, Sammy didn't have a chance to make it.

Then Tim began tossing in remarks as well. At last with a final taunt that the Mystery Club was for losers and kids and they were sure glad they had better things to do with their time, Butch and Tim ran out of air.

Butch wasn't quite ready to call it quits though. Directly behind Sammy a large half-frozen pool of water had formed in a low spot on the playground. Sammy couldn't see it because his back was turned, but Butch could and so could Tim. Their eyes met over Sammy's head, then Butch edged forward. Lightly he pushed his fist into Sammy's ribs, then flicked the back of his hand against Sammy's cheek.

Naturally, Sammy backed up a couple of paces.

Again Butch's fist brushed Sammy's midsection, slightly harder this time.

Sammy took two more steps backward.

Butch and Tim had played this game before. Butch would force Sammy back three or four more steps, then Tim would put out his foot. There would be no way Sammy could avoid ending up flat on his back in the icy water.

"You guys are just lucky none of the kids in our class want to join that sissy club of yours," Butch went on, deliberately holding Sammy's attention so he wouldn't realize what was planned. "If we did you'd be so far outclassed you wouldn't know what hit you."

Two more steps—

But before Butch could encourage Sammy to take them, he felt himself being swung around from behind.

"You wanna make a bet?" Windy Jackson asked, looming in front of Butch.

Sammy felt a flood of relief. All he could think of was taking off and getting out of there while he had the chance. He took two quick steps, but then he stopped. Windy had come to his rescue. What kind of a guy would he be if he ran for cover and left Windy on his own with these two bullies?

Straightening his shoulders he moved back to face Butch and Tim, but he could feel the colour creeping into his cheeks. Windy had been watching him pretty closely. There was no way Windy could have missed seeing his fear and guessing that he'd almost run away. What if he said something and made fun of him?

Sammy forced himself to look up. For a fraction of a second his glance met Windy's.

To his relief, instead of seeing disappointment in Windy's expression, he saw understanding.

Again he looked down, pretending to be digging in the snow for something, because that would really fix things if Butch Ogrodnick caught him getting all choked up.

But before Butch had time to notice anything, Windy challenged, "If you guys think you're such mystery hotshots, how about a little contest?"

From the moment that Windy had appeared Butch had started losing some of his self-confidence. Two against one was the kind of odds he liked—or even better, three against one. Two against two with Windy Jackson on the opposing team was something else. As far as Butch was concerned it was time to split.

Windy, however, had other ideas. "Since you think you're so great at solving mysteries," he went on, "we'll give you a chance to show off. We'll make you a bet—that our Mystery Club can solve the best mystery your whole class can put together, and that we can write one that you won't be able to solve in a million years."

All thought of retreating was forgotten. Butch threw back his head and guffawed. "You're on, man. What are the stakes?"

"Losers have to be slaves to the winners for a week," Windy suggested.

Butch's eyes widened for a moment, then he nodded. With a sign to Tim to follow, he headed off across the playground to inform the rest of the class about the great contest he'd lined up.

Sammy watched them in silence for a moment then turned to Windy. He wanted to tell him how he felt, only he was too embarrassed. "Thanks," he managed.

"Hey, man, for what? You were doing just fine. Come on. Let's go break the news to the club." And as if the whole thing was already forgotten, Windy strode off toward the corner of the field where a pick-up field hockey match was in progress.

Laura, Kathy, Sven, Tony and Mike were all playing. Windy waited for a break in the action, then moved into the middle of the field. "Guess what, you guys? We're entering a contest," he announced casually.

There was dead silence for a moment after he finished explaining. Then Laura said disbelievingly, "You mean the Mystery Club has to make good on that dumb bet and beat Mr. Carlysle's class or be their slaves for a whole week!" Her voice rose in anguish at the thought.

Windy nodded.

Mike was looking thoughtfully from Windy's face to Sammy's. "I don't suppose you'd like to tell us just how this all came about would you?" he asked.

"What does it matter?" Windy blustered. As he spoke he moved so his body seemed to be partially excluding Sammy from the conversation. "We were just talking, and we got the idea for a contest—"

Sammy moved out from behind him. "Windy did it to get me out of a jam," he said in a quiet voice. In a few brief sentences he described exactly what had happened.

"Don't listen to him. He was doing just fine without any help," Windy protested. "Anyway, what's it matter how it got started? The important thing is that we've got to win this contest, or the whole rest of our lives we'll be forced to eat all the humble pie that Butch Ogrodnick wants to serve us."

Laura and Kathy groaned.

For a moment Mike ignored them. He was still looking at Windy, a mixture of approval and surprise in his expression, and for a moment Sammy thought he was going to make some comment. But he must have changed his mind, because he just turned to the girls and said brightly, "The contest's a great idea! Cut the gloom and doom! There's no way anybody in Mr. Carlysle's room is going to beat us at our own game. We've been thinking mystery ever since last September, while they've never even considered it before. We'll lick them easily.''

Laura didn't share his enthusiasm. "What if Mr. Carlysle helps make theirs up?" she asked.

"Which he will," Windy put in quickly. "Butch needs all the help he can get."

For an instant the sunshine in Mike's expression dimmed slightly, but almost immediately it was back. "So, big deal. We'll get Mr. Proctor to help us." And as if that settled the problem, he reached for a couple of hockey sticks that had been left as extras on the snow. He tossed one to Windy and another to Sammy, then announced that the field hockey game was again underway.

Next afternoon when the final bell rang, Mike, Tony, Laura, Kathy, Sammy and Windy all remained in their places. They waited while the other students tidied their desks and disappeared into the hallway, then they got to their feet and approached Mr. Proctor's desk.

He looked up inquiringly.

Mike had been appointed spokesperson. As he explained what had happened on the playground a smile came into Mr. Proctor's eyes. But as Mike finished with the request for help, Mr. Proctor shook his head.

"You mean you won't help us make up a mystery?" Mike blurted out before he could stop himself.

The corners of Mr. Proctor's mouth quavered disobediently. "What happened to all those enterprising kids I spoke to last December when the club was in danger of being closed down?"

Mike struggled to hide his impatience. This was no time for one of Mr. Proctor's games. "The other class has already admitted they're going to get Mr. Carlysle to help them." He left the rest of the argument unstated.

Mr. Proctor regarded them in silence for a moment, then got to his feet and moved toward the window. For several seconds he stared out at the playground. Just as the silence was beginning to get uncomfortable, he turned back and said evenly, "If you want me to help you, I will. However . . ."

The rest of what he had to say was drowned under a chorus of hoorays.

He waited for quiet to be restored, then continued in the same even tone, "However, I think upon reflection you will decide that you don't want that."

There was stunned silence.

At last, enlightenment crept over Mike's face. "You're right," he said. "If they have to admit they need help, they've got a problem. Come on, guys.'' And he led the way out into the corridor.

A look of satisfaction crossed Mr. Proctor's face as he watched them go.

"Whose side goes first, theirs or ours?" Mike asked as soon as they were in the hallway.

"Ours." Windy lifted his chin so his bristly butch cut stood taller. "You shouldn't have let Mr. Proctor off the hook. He'd already said he'd help if we really wanted him to—''

"We don't," Laura and Kathy chorused. "How are we going to prove we really are the best mystery buffs in Canville Elementary if we need help?"

Windy's chin continued to jut out. "Better not to prove it than to be slaves to those bozos for a whole week! That's what's going to happen if we don't have Mr. Proctor to help us." They'd reached the street by this time. There was a pebble on the edge of the curb half embedded in snow. Windy gave it an angry kick. "There's no way we're gonna be able to make up a mystery that'll fool thirty-two people," he finished glumly.

Silence greeted his remark. He had a point. Where were they going to get a mystery good enough to fool an entire class? To make things worse, where were they going to get one in just five days?

"How about that newspaper Citizenship Award story of yours?" Mike suggested at last.

Windy stopped scowling. He rubbed his chin. "You know, that just might work," he said thoughtfully.

"What's that story?" Sammy asked. "I've never heard it."

"Neither have I," Laura agreed.

Windy shook his head. "Wait till Wednesday," he said with a self-satisfied grin. Then, shoving his hands into his pockets and straightening his shoulders, he sauntered off as if once again in full control of the universe.

The following Wednesday the library was so crowded there was hardly room for everyone to sit down. Every student from Mr. Carlysle's room was present, together with all the members of the Mystery Club. But while the guests had come primed to listen intently to every word and ask lots of questions, the club members had been given strict instructions to keep quiet no matter what. There was no way they were to say anything that might help the other side work out the mystery.

Mike moved to the front of the room. Just as he was about to explain the rules of the challenge match and welcome the visitors, two latecomers appeared in the doorway: Mr. Carlysle followed by Mr. Proctor.

As they moved into the two comfortable seats vacated for them by Sven and Sammy, Mr. Proctor glanced casually at Mike. He raised one hand with his forefinger extended and tipped an imaginary cap.

It was all Mike could do not to burst out laughing. Mr. Proctor was giving the SEP sign for good luck! No one else in the room, however, noticed the gesture.

"Welcome to the first session of our mystery match-up," Mike began when at last everyone was seated. "It's our turn today to present . . ." The words dried in his throat, for to his dismay the room was rocking with laughter. Flustered, he looked around. Then his concern evaporated as he discovered the cause. Standing in the library doorway wearing a bright red wet suit, was Windy. He had huge black flippers on his feet, and over his eyes a large pair of underwater goggles. They were so big that all that could be seen of his face was a small patch from cheekbone to chin.

He advanced into the room with wide-spaced steps, struggling with each one to find sufficient floor space for the flippers. At last he reached the front. He put his notes on the lectern, pushed the goggles onto his forehead and gazed along the rows of listeners. When he located Butch and Tim sprawled at the end of the third row, he straightened his shoulders and thrust out his chin.

It was a mistake. The movement dislodged the goggles and they fell back down over his face. He pushed at them a second time, but they fell down again.

By this time the room was laughing even harder.

Windy conceded defeat. Grinning sheepishly, he raised his eyes skyward for a moment, then pulled the goggles down around his neck.

A round of applause came from the section where the Mystery Club members were seated.

"My mystery takes place in a small town in southern Alberta," Windy began, as soon as the room was quiet.

"That's foothill country and range land, not seashore," a voice protested. "So how come the costume?"

A tinge of pink crept into Windy's cheeks. He shifted the goggles so they weren't directly under his chin. "Be patient, okay? It's part of the story. You'll understand in a minute." He glanced back down at his notes.

"The newspaper in this small town was in

financial trouble. To build up readership the editor decided to hold a special Citizenship Award contest and offer $500 to someone in the area who had done something really outstanding. The idea was that people would write down what they had done, or what one of their friends had done, and send it in. The stories would be published and the best one would win the award. Of course the stories had to be absolutely true—no exaggerations." Windy could feel Mike grinning at that remark, and he kept his eyes focussed on his notes.

"Dozens of entries were received. Some were about people who had rescued cats from the top of trees; some were about people who had reported fires that had broken out when no one was home. A couple were about people who did volunteer work in the community. But two stood out well above the others: one about a lady who jumped into the river in the late fall to save a little boy from drowning, and the other about a man who had helped an old prospector rescue his life's savings."

Windy paused and looked around the room.

"A lot of the committee thought the lady deserved the award because this wasn't a run-of-the-mill rescue. In the first place it had taken place in November when the river was icy cold, and in the second, the lady who'd done the rescuing was over seventy years of age.

"The rest, however, favoured the letter from this guy Dinnigan, who'd helped the old prospector.

"Nobody knew Dinnigan very well. He'd come from the Coast just a few weeks before. As a matter of fact, he had arrived in town at just about the time that the $500 contest was first being advertised."

"Now I get the costume!" a voice called from the back. "He was a deep-sea diver. Right?"

"Sort of," Windy agreed. "Only not one of those divers who use oxygen tanks. Dinnigan was a deep-sea pearl diver, and he prided himself on being able to hold his breath for so long that he didn't need oxygen."

"How long could he hold it?" a girl from Mr. Carlysle's class asked.

"He claimed he could hold it for three minutes without even trying, and for four if he really had to," Windy replied.

A succession of sharp intakes of air sounded from all over the library as various listeners started timing themselves to see how long they could hold their breath.

"According to Dinnigan, that was why he'd been able to help the old prospector," Windy went on.

"Come again?" Butch retorted, his voice heavy with sarcasm.

"I'll read you the story Dinnigan sent in to the newspaper," Windy explained.

"Last fall I was on a hunting and fishing trip out in the woods," he read. "After supper one evening I noticed this big fire a half kilometre or so away, so I figured I'd better check it out. I headed over and found a wooden cabin going up in smoke and an old prospector standing by with tears streaming down his cheeks.

"All of a sudden he got this stricken look on his face. 'My savings!' he gasped, and before I realized what was happening he grabbed the kerosene lantern I was carrying and started racing back toward the burning cabin.

"I raced after him and grabbed his arm. 'What's wrong?' I yelled.

" 'My savings!' he cried again. 'In there!' Apparently he hadn't much faith in banks, and had kept his life savings hidden up in the rafters of the cabin in a tin box.

"By this time the cabin was so full of smoke nobody could breathe in there. The old guy would have suffocated in no time if he'd tried to get in. So I told him I'd go instead.

"I took back the kerosene lantern and headed for the cabin. I knew that if the box was as well hidden as the old guy claimed, I'd never find it in the thick smoke without a light.

"At the doorway I almost stopped and turned back, because it looked really hopeless. It was even worse than I'd imagined. The smoke was so thick it was impossible to see anything. But thinking of the poor old guy losing his life savings made me go on.

"I turned up the wick of the lantern as high as it would go so I'd get as much light as possible, took a huge lungful of air and plunged into the swirling grey darkness.

"It was sure a good thing I'd brought that lantern. Even with it turned up to its brightest I could still hardly see through the smoke, and it took me four minutes and fifteen seconds to locate the box way up in the rafters and pry it loose.

"My lungs were bursting. I'd never held my breath that long before, and I knew I couldn't hold it much longer. I couldn't take time to climb back down from the rafters. Clutching the box under my arm I crossed my fingers and jumped.

"For a second after I landed I thought I

must have broken something—every bone screamed with pain. But I was more worried about the fact that I was starting to black out. I'd been without air for too long. With one last terrific effort I dove for the door, and the next thing I knew I was lying outside on the ground, sucking in great gasps of cool night air, with the old prospector's life savings safely clutched under my arm.''

Windy stopped reading. He looked over the rows of listeners. ''The committee was pretty impressed with Dinnigan's letter. The only thing that worried them was that they couldn't find the old prospector to corroborate the story. In fact, no one else had even known about the fire. But that was no reason to doubt Dinnigan, they decided, so they took a vote, and Dinnigan won out over the lady.

''The newspaper editor was about to call Dinnigan and tell him he'd won when one of the junior reporters whispered something in his ear.

'' 'What do you mean something in Dinnigan's story doesn't sound right?' the editor thundered, because he didn't appreciate being whispered at by junior reporters.

''Again the junior reporter whispered.

''The editor stopped glowering. He told the committee what the junior reporter had said.

"A new vote was taken and this time the committee voted unanimously in favour of giving the award to the lady, and suggesting to Dinnigan that he find somewhere else to live because he wasn't the sort of citizen their town wanted."

Windy paused. His gaze travelled over the rows of listeners. When it reached the section where Mr. Carlysle's class was sitting, he said, "What did the junior reporter notice in Dinnigan's story that gave him away?" He couldn't resist stressing the word junior so Butch and Tim would know just how highly he rated their mystery-solving abilities.

He was watching them closely. To his delight neither of them knew the answer. Nor for a moment did anyone else, and the Mystery Club members held their breath. But just as they were thinking Mr. Carlysle's room might concede defeat, Julie Thomas, a blonde-haired girl in the second row, raised her hand.

What was Julie's answer? Turn to page 152 and see if you are right.

Science Fair

The score stood one to nothing in favour of Mr. Carlysle's class when the challenge match resumed the following Wednesday.

"Come on, you guys. Up with the smarts, okay?" Windy urged the other club members as they filed through the library doorway and headed for the front row of seats.

"Right on," Mike agreed. "Those guys got our mystery last week, so we've got to get theirs. Otherwise we're going to look pretty stupid." He sat down between Tony and Laura.

"Who cares about stupid?" Tony countered. "What's worrying me is the thought of having to be slaves for a week to people like Butch Ogrodnick and Tim Silverstein." As he spoke he glanced across the room at the two heavy-set figures who had just entered. Both Butch and Tim were a good five kilos heavier than any of the other grade fives and half a head taller. "I can just see those guys making us scrub the sidewalk in front of their houses with a toothbrush."

"And while we scrub they'll probably be tossing eggs or tomatoes on the part we've just cleaned," Mike agreed with a grin.

But Laura was thinking of other things. "What do you think their mystery will be about? If Mr. Carlysle helped them—"

"Which he did," Tony said in a voice of doom. "I was talking to some of the kids from their class yesterday. Get practising with those toothbrushes, because no matter what their mystery is about, it's going to be tough."

As Tony was talking Mike tilted back his chair and brushed a hand casually through his unruly brown hair. "Come on, you guys," he said in his cheeriest manner. "What's to worry? We're the mystery experts, remember? We'll have no problem." But even to his ears the words had a slightly artificial ring.

It took several moments for all of Mr. Carlysle's class to find places to sit in the crowded room. Then Belinda Tanaka, notes in hand, made her way to the front. She was all dressed up for the occasion in a trim-fitting black skirt and a long-sleeved white blouse. She was so much shorter than any of the other grade fives that only her face could be seen over top of the lectern.

"Our mystery takes place at a Provincial Elementary School Science Fair," Belinda began in a clear, high-pitched voice.

"Is it a true story?" Tony asked quickly. The Mystery Club members had agreed ahead of time that it was important to get all the extra information they could as the story went along.

Belinda nodded. "It happened when Mr. Carlysle was teaching at a small school in northern British Columbia."

Laura's eyebrows raised in resignation as she glanced at Mike. "There goes the ball game," she murmured under her breath.

Mike forced a reassuring grin. "No way," he whispered back, but to be honest he felt much more like groaning.

"It's about a grade five Science class in a school called Bennington Elementary," Belinda went on, consulting her notes for a moment. "Bennington was pretty small by city standards, but it had a fantastic Science program, organized by one of the best Science teachers in the whole province. Unfortunately, the school district was having money problems. So in an effort to cut costs the District Board decided to reduce the number of Science programs. Those at small schools like Bennington were to be dropped, and the students would be bussed to larger schools for their Science classes. In Bennington's case the students were to go to Westbank Elementary, twenty-five kilometres away."

A chorus of groans forced Belinda to pause for a minute. The audience held firm opinions on bussing. Only a few weeks earlier some of them had faced that very same threat when their French Immersion classes had been considered too small, and they had only escaped being bussed to a larger school through the eloquence of Mr. Tate at a School Board meeting.

"Of course the Bennington parents and students protested," Belinda went on. "They urged the Board to reconsider and to let their Science program continue. Finally the School Board agreed to let the decision rest on the Science Fair, which was scheduled for mid-January. If Bennington could prove by their submission that their Science program measured up well against the programs offered by the other schools in the province, then the Board would agree to let it continue.

"When Mr. Henckleman, Bennington's Science teacher, heard the Board's statement he said their program was as good as dead. There was no way a small school could put together a project that could compete against projects from large city schools. They had neither the funds to finance it, nor the equipment to carry it through.

"But a couple of Bennington's top Science students came up with an idea. They suggested that the class should do a water study. Not a study of mineral content or anything like that, because the school didn't have the equipment to do those tests properly. They'd study growth potential to show how well the water from various regions could support fish life and water plants. It would be an inexpensive study because they could get water samples from various lakes and rivers across Canada, and the fish and plant life could be collected for nothing from one of their fishing areas."

"What a neat study!" Sammy Jack exclaimed. "I wish we could do something like that!"

Belinda smiled at him. "Mr. Henckleman liked the suggestion too. The only question was whether or not they would have time to do a proper growth study. But it was only October, so he decided it would be all right.

"First off they had to get the water samples. Since they didn't have much money they decided to enlist some help. They made a list of all the places across Canada where the grade five students had relatives and picked out the names of those who lived near a river, or a lake or a pond. Then they wrote letters explaining about their Science project and asked for a sealed container of water from that particular area.

"While they were waiting for replies they turned their attention to collecting the fish and plant life they would need. With Mr. Henckleman's help they organized a field trip to one of the local fishing lakes and brought back several jars of water lily sprouts ready for planting, and more than a hundred live minnows.

"Early in November the water samples started coming back. Some had to be discarded because they came from locations too close together, but before long they had eight really good ones. Four were from rivers: the Thompson, the Bow, the North Saskatchewan, and the MacKenzie. The rest were from lakes: Lake Manitoba, Gull Lake, Lake Superior, and Lake Ontario."

"Where's Gull Lake?" Tony asked sharply.

"In Alberta," Belinda answered.

"Come on! Don't give them clues!" Butch protested, glaring at Belinda.

Belinda glared right back. "I'm not," she protested. "If you think that's a clue then maybe you're not as smart as you think you are.''

Ignoring Butch she returned her attention to her story. "They set the eight water samples out on a long table, and pasted labels on each container stating where the water had come from. Then into each one they put several water lily shoots and a dozen live minnows.''

Sammy was frowning. "There's no way," he objected, "that they could expect the minnows to live in containers like that. In the first place they'd need food, and in the second, they'd need changes of water.'' His face was serious. "Fish would use up the oxygen in even a big jar in a matter of days.''

"That's right," Belinda agreed. "Every day the Bennington students added fish food to the containers. Every second day they hooked up the air jets that Mr. Henckleman had provided to oxygenate the water. And every fourth day they estimated the size of the lilies in each container, the growth, energy level and appetite of the fish and registered their findings on a detailed chart.''

Over Sammy's head Mike exchanged a pleased look with Laura. If this mystery of Mr. Carlysle's class was going to be about wildlife and nature, then thank goodness the Mystery Club had Sammy on its side.

"Was there a difference, when they registered their measurements?" Sammy asked.

"Not right away. But after a couple of weeks it was obvious that the water from some areas was going to prove to be better for supporting fish and plant life than the water from others.

"Of course, when the class discovered this they got really excited. It was still another six weeks until the Science Fair, and by then the difference in growth potential would be even more remarkable. Surely, the students reasoned, the Science Fair officials would be impressed, and would allow the Bennington Science program to continue after all.

"Only," and Belinda's voice dropped a notch, "early in December, Bennington's hopes plummeted. Westbank had learned of their project. Determined to beat them, Westbank decided not only to do a similar study, but a better one. They found a well-protected inland lake where there were still lots of minnows, and even managed to find some water lily plants that were still growing. Then, since money was no problem, they wrote to municipal offices all across the country, asked for water samples and paid for them.

"They realized they'd have to work quickly. They would need a good four weeks in order to allow sufficient growing time to make their results significant, and already it was early December. But as long as they were ready to start soon after December 15 they'd be all right.

"Then for a minute it looked as if they were going to be out of luck after all, because they had forgotten about the Christmas mailing rush when they'd estimated how long it would take to get their samples back. It was December 22 when the last one arrived. But the very next day they had their study going, and that same afternoon two Westbank kids made a special trip over to Bennington to boast that the smaller school might as well give up."

There was dead silence as Belinda paused to consult her notes.

"Things couldn't have looked bleaker for Bennington," she continued. "But two days later a girl from the Science project met those same two Westbank students when she was shopping. Again they started bragging about how they were going to beat Bennington at the Science Fair and the girl got mad. 'How do you know you are?' she demanded. 'How do you know your study is any better than ours?'

" 'Because we've got water samples from much better places,' the Westbank students replied smugly. 'Yours are just from dull places, but ours are chosen from right across Canada—Georgia Strait, the Strait of Juan de Fuca, the Bay of Fundy, Red River, Lake Ontario, Lake Superior, Hudson Bay and the lower St. Lawrence.'

"Instead of being discouraged, the Bennington girl was delighted. 'We can stop worrying,' she told the rest of the class the next day. 'There's no way Westbank is going to beat us. In fact, in about two more days I bet they'll announce that they've decided not to enter a water study in the Science Fair after all. What's the point if more than half of it is going to have to be thrown out?'

"The rest of the class were gazing at her as if she was crazy, so she told them what the Westbank students had said."

Belinda looked up from her notes. She glanced at Mr. Carlysle as if for confirmation that she'd covered all the points. "That's our mystery," she said finally. "How did this girl know that Westbank's water study wouldn't win the Science Fair?"

Several of the Mystery Club members looked thoroughly puzzled, but Mike was grinning broadly. He raised his hand.

What was Mike's answer? Turn to page 153 and see if you are right.

Balloon Race Mystery

It was cold and windy as Mike and Tony came out into the schoolyard after the Mystery Club meeting was over.

Mike tugged the maroon and white toque he was wearing farther down over his ears and pushed the zipper a little higher on his ski jacket. "I was thinking about Belinda's Science Fair mystery," he said. "That growth study business was really interesting. Did you know that a single minnow can have up to a thousand babies?"

"Is that right?" Tony replied. Then struggling to keep his face serious, he added, "I wonder if she has trouble finding a baby-sitter."

Mike's eyes lifted skyward as if appealing for help, then he thrust one foot sideways across the snow. Tony sidestepped neatly.

"So, now what?" Mike went on as if there had been no interruption. "We got their mystery, and they got ours. We're tied. Nobody proved anything.''

"Wrong," Tony corrected. "We proved something. In fact we proved two things— that we could win without help, and that they couldn't.''

"Humph! Try to tell them that.''

"That's the third thing we proved," Tony added.

"Come again?''

"We also proved that we're smart—smart enough not to go around telling people as big as Butch Ogrodnick that we beat them.''

It was Mike's turn to grin. "Do you think maybe we should offer them a return match?''

"And set ourselves up a second time for that sidewalk toothbrush duty? Are you crazy?''

"Then how do we convince them that we aren't as dumb and kindergartenish as they said? Don't forget that's what started this whole thing.''

"Butch and Tim are the only two who think that way and who cares what those two bozos think?''

"I do," Mike said firmly.

"And so do we," a voice said from behind them.

With the noise that the wind had been

making, and the fact that their toques were pulled well down over their ears, neither Mike nor Tony had heard anyone approaching. Now they turned to find Windy and Sammy Jack directly behind them. Mike glanced quickly at Tony, hoping his surprise didn't show. As a rule Sammy headed off by himself as soon as school was over.

"Somebody's got to take down those guys," Windy went on. "Let's call for a return match, and this time make sure we beat them."

Tony's eyebrows lifted. "Great." The word was heavy with sarcasm. "I thought that was what we were trying to do last time."

If Windy noticed the sarcasm he gave no sign of it. "They'll have to go first this time—it's only fair in a return match. That means we'll have the final go, and that's where we'll beat them because Sammy's got a terrific mystery ready."

Attention shifted from Windy to the slender dark-haired boy standing beside him.

"Is that true? Do you have a mystery ready?" Mike asked.

Sammy nodded.

"A good one?"

The attention was making Sammy self-conscious. He looked down at the ground. "I dunno—I think so," he said softly.

"You haven't been talked into it, have you?" Mike asked warily. He was eyeing Windy. It wasn't like Sammy to volunteer to speak to a whole group of people if he didn't have to. As a rule in school he preferred to let someone else do the talking.

Sammy shook his head. "I got us into this. I should help get us out."

Windy couldn't resist a self-satisfied smirk. He'd guessed what Mike had been thinking.

A resigned sigh came from Tony's direction. "That sounds as if you guys really intend to go ahead with this return match. Who's going to tell Butch and Tim? Any volunteers?" From the sound of his voice it was obvious he was picturing a future of endless toothbrush duty.

"We will," Windy replied, and before either Mike or Tony could object, he and Sammy moved off across the playground.

Mr. Carlysle's class must have been as eager as Mike and Windy to prove who was tops at mystery solving, because they jumped at the chance of a rematch. The following Wednesday all thirty-two students from Mr. Carlysle's class, the Mystery Club members, and more than a dozen guests who had learned of the challenge assembled in the library.

As Windy pushed his way into the crowded room he groaned. "The biggest mystery we're all gonna have to solve today," he complained, "is how to find enough air in here to stay alive." As he spoke he was elbowing his way past several of Mr. Carlysle's class. They exchanged amused glances, but Windy was too busy pushing to notice.

A chubby, round-faced boy named Denton took his place at the lectern. "Our mystery is about a balloon race," he began as soon as the room was quiet.

"Do you think Mr. Carlysle helped them again?" Laura whispered to Mike who was sitting beside her in the front row.

"I know he did. He told Mr. Proctor he was going to."

Laura's eyebrows lifted resignedly.

"This special balloon race is being held to mark the 205th anniversary of the launching of the first balloon," Denton continued, reading from his carefully prepared notes. "The Montgolfier brothers got the idea first. They made a big balloon and filled it with smoke from a straw fire."

"Did it actually fly?" Tony asked.

"Right up into the clouds," Denton answered.

"You mean everyone in this race has to do

that? Fill a balloon over a bonfire?'' Tony's voice rose in disbelief.

Denton grinned. "No. They just have to use hot air.''

Tony wiped imaginary beads of perspiration from his forehead. "That's good!''

"How does a hot air balloon work?" Kathy Chiu asked.

Denton glanced questioningly at Butch and Tim.

"Go ahead and tell 'em,'' Butch drawled lazily. "Give 'em all the help they want. They'll never get this anyway.'' With a smug grin he settled deeper into his chair.

"A balloon flies,'' Denton explained, "when what is inside the balloon is lighter than the air outside. This is easy if you use hydrogen or helium like they did later on because both gases are lighter than air. But the first balloonists had to depend on heating the air to make the balloon rise. The more the air was heated, the higher the balloon went. If the heat was turned off, the balloon fell.''

"Hey! Hot air rises! We learned that in Science!'' Windy remarked with sudden enlightenment.

Butch gave him a pitying look.

Sven Olafsen had been listening to Denton's explanation with growing excitement. Leaning past Kathy he caught Tony's eye.

"That doesn't sound so tough. Do you figure maybe we should try that?"

Before Tony could answer Mike said, "If I were you, Tony, I'd let Sven go first. Maybe getting the balloon to go up isn't too much of a problem, but there's something about that word 'falls' that I'm not so crazy about."

Denton heard the exchange. He laughed. "You're right. But you've got a few extras to help you—like the outlet valve at the top, and the rip panel in the side, and all that ballast that you can toss overboard whenever you—"

"Cancel the scientific lecture, okay?" Butch interrupted impatiently. "Anything else they need to know they can ask as you go along."

Denton coughed to hide his embarrassment, then continued, "The route for this special 205th anniversary balloon race is from an isolated little French village near the coast, across the English Channel, to a flat open field directly over top of the highest, sheerest section of the famous White Cliffs of Dover." He paused a moment, then added, "And that makes it tough."

"Why?" Laura asked in a puzzled tone.

Most of the Mystery Club members had been wondering the same thing and they waited eagerly for Denton's answer.

"Because at the start of a trip it's pretty

easy to get extra height when you want it. You've got ballast you can jettison, or you can turn the heat up full under the balloon. But by the end of a trip, particularly one that involves crossing thirty or more kilometres of ocean and fighting winds and sudden drops in altitude all the way, the balloonists will have already jettisoned most of their ballast and used up most of their fuel. By the time they sight the coast of England, if they suddenly discover they're sailing in too low, they might not be able to make that final climb.''

He paused for a moment to see if there were any more questions. When there weren't, he continued, ''The rules of the race state that each balloon must be an authentic hot air balloon. No modern equipment can be added, with the exception of a CB radio for emergency purposes. Each balloon will carry one of those, but everything else has to be exactly as it was in the early days of balloon racing.''

Mike leaned forward in his chair. ''How many balloons are entered?''

''Twelve. They're from different countries —Germany, England, France, a couple from the United States, even one from Canada. There are also a few independent balloons with crews of mixed nationality.''

"Is there a favourite?" Mike went on, still leaning forward.

Denton smiled. "Actually there is. It's the Canadian balloon, flown by Captain Gordon McBain of Toronto, and his twelve-year-old twins, Daphne and Todd."

"You mean kids can enter?" Windy asked.

"If they're experienced, and the McBain twins are. They've been flying balloons with their dad ever since they were little. In Captain McBain's opinion they are the best crew he could possibly have."

A murmur of interested chatter greeted this remark.

"But not all the teams are experienced," Denton went on. "Some of the independents don't seem to know much about ballooning at all. There's one team flying a blue and green balloon that the other crews find it hard not to laugh at. Not only are they totally clued out about what they're doing, but their balloon is twice as big as everybody else's and they can hardly control it."

There was a laugh from the audience at the picture Denton had painted.

"The reason the race is starting from a remote little village is to ensure security," Denton went on. "The officials want to make sure that no one can sneak in and tamper with any of the valuable balloons. They also want to make sure their special display of prizes is safe. Not only is the prize for this year's race on display, the prizes for all the races for the next ten years are also there. Every prize is a brick of solid gold, weighing thirty-two kilograms.

"The officials decided to bring all ten gold bricks as an advertising stunt to build interest in the international event, and they have succeeded. Newspapers from all over the world have carried stories about it.

"As soon as the race starts the display will be dismantled, one of the bricks will be flown to Dover ready to greet the winning balloon crew when the race is over. The other nine will be returned to a Swiss bank where they will remain until race time next year.

"But," and Denton's voice dropped ominously, "the very evening before the race is to be held, the display of gold bricks disappears."

A sharp intake of breath came from somewhere near the end of the front row, and everyone laughed.

"The police are baffled. How can the gold bricks have disappeared when no one from outside has been allowed into the starting site, and none of the balloon crews have been allowed to leave? Obviously the bricks must still be somewhere in the area, the police decide, and they begin to search.

"They start with the contestants' living quarters. When nothing is found there they head down to the launch site to search inside the balloons. But as soon as they reach the launch site they realize that the mystery is solved. One of the balloon mooring pads is standing empty. And while the police are still debating what to do, the missing balloon sails into sight high overhead—the red and white Canadian balloon.

"While they wait for the balloon to land the police check with the security guards. As they suspected, the Canadian balloon is the only one that has been off the ground in the past twenty-four hours. According to the security guards, it headed off, shooting up into the air so quickly and gaining so much altitude that they could hardly believe it. Then it disappeared and was gone for over an hour.

"Long enough to have taken the gold bars to some safe distant hiding spot, the police realize.

"The moment the balloon touches ground, they seize Captain McBain. He tries to explain that he was checking a new lifting manoeuvre. That was why he had been flying so high, he says, to make sure the rigging was properly regulated so he would be able to make that final climb to the top of the White Cliffs.

"The police don't believe him. They insist the reason he was flying so high was to avoid detection.

" 'Don't you realize that's the proof that I couldn't have taken—'

"The police don't even let him finish. They bustle him into a police car and take him off to prison.

"Daphne and Todd are stunned. For hours they agonize over what they should do. At last they decide that they should go ahead with the race and try to win for their dad's sake. As soon as it's over, they'll get to work to prove his innocence."

Denton gazed out over the rows of listeners. "Next morning when Todd and Daphne start preparing their balloon for take-off, the other balloonists try to stop them. 'It's too dangerous!' they exclaim. But Todd and Daphne pay no attention. They know exactly what to do.

"Well ahead of take-off time they start heating the air in the large balloon cavity, but they take care to heat it only so much. Then they reduce the heat and keep the temperature constant. They don't want to take a chance on being disqualified for taking off too early. But as soon as the starting signal is given, they increase the heat once again. At the same time they jettison a small amount of ballast to start their ascent.

"Now the trick is to balance the heat applied to the air inside the balloon cavity with the decrease in air pressure outside as they rise skyward. Insufficient heat will stop their ascent. But too much could take them up too quickly, and if that happens they'll suffer exactly the same 'bends' that deep sea divers have to guard against.

"At last they are high enough to level off. They reduce the heat slightly, open the top valve so a sudden drop in air pressure outside won't cause the balloon to shoot skyward, then relax and look around to see how the other balloonists are doing. Most are flying fairly close to the Canadians, but one balloon is barely skimming the white-capped waves. It's the blue and green balloon crewed by the two men who didn't seem to know much about ballooning.

"Todd and Daphne stare down and watch. 'Boy, are they clued out,' Todd says as the two men with the huge blue and green balloon jettison like crazy. Even their heavy jackets and boots are going overboard, yet the balloon is continuing to lose altitude.

" 'Do you think they've forgotten to turn their heat up high enough?' Daphne suggests.

'With that huge balloon they probably need to use more heat than the rest of us.' She's starting to get worried, for if the blue and green balloon sinks much lower it could be right in the ocean.

" 'Either that or they've forgotten to close their top valve,' Todd puts in.

"Some of the other balloonists must have been thinking the same thing. At that moment, over their CB radio, Todd and Daphne hear **one** of the other teams telling the struggling balloon crew to do just that. But there is no reaction from the blue and green balloon. It just dips closer to the angry waves.

" 'That proves how inexperienced they are,' Todd says disgustedly. 'They don't even know enough to keep their radio turned on. But it's okay. There's the coast of England right ahead. All they've got to do is swing away from the White Cliffs and land on that bit of beach over there. They'll lose the race of course, for not landing at the proper finish line, but at least they'll be safe.'

"Daphne directs the binoculars toward the coast. Sure enough to the left is an area where there is flat sandy beach. Todd is right—the struggling balloonists will be fine if they head there.

"But Todd is now worried about their own

performance. 'Come on, Daph,' he urges. 'Forget about those other people and concentrate on us. We've got to get some height.' He points to the solid walls of white that loom directly in front of them. 'Jettison the rest of the ballast while I turn up the heat!'

"But Daphne continues to peer through the binoculars at the balloon below. 'Their top valve isn't open,' she says in a puzzled tone, more to herself than to her brother. 'It doesn't make sense. There has to be reason why—'

" 'Come on, Daph! I thought you wanted to help Dad.'

"At last Daphne moves, but not to do what her brother expects. Instead of jettisoning ballast, she reaches up and pulls the cord that opens the outlet valve at the top of the balloon. Immediately hot air rushes out and the balloon starts descending.

" 'What are you doing! Cut that out!' Todd shouts.

"Daphne continues to hold the valve open.

" 'For Pete's sake, Daph—!'

" 'You said we were to help Dad. Well, if we take time to finish the race we'll be too late. We've got to stop those two men. Don't you remember what Dad was trying to tell the police, that there was no way he could have—'

"Daphne doesn't have to finish for Todd understands. Grabbing the CB he radios to the police, then he sets to work to help his sister get the balloon down quickly. While she controls the flow of air out of the exit valve, he opens the rip panel, and as soon as they are almost down he drops the thick manila drag rope over the side to act as an extra brake.

"Moments later they are on the ground, landing not more than twenty metres from the blue and green balloon.

"When the crew members see Todd and Daphne approaching they look pretty unfriendly. 'What d'you kids want?' they bellow.

"Todd swallows hard. 'The gold bricks,' he manages, 'so my dad can get out of jail.'

"The bigger of the two men gets to his feet. He's grinning, only it's not a pleasant grin. But at that minute the police helicopter sails into sight. The grin gives way to alarm. There's no way the men can escape, however, and they know it. When the helicopter lands they give up."

Denton looked up from his notes. "That's the mystery. How did Daphne and Todd know the crew of the blue and green balloon had stolen the gold?"

For the past couple of minutes Butch had

been leaning forward in his chair, leering at Windy and the Mystery Club members, obviously convinced that the challenge match was already won. But as half a dozen Mystery Club members put their hands in the air the leer was replaced by a stunned expression.

What did the club members answer? Turn to page 154 and see if you are right.

The Buffalo Stone

The second half of the return challenge match was scheduled for the following Wednesday.

"Do you think Sammy's mystery is going to be good enough to stump Mr. Carlysle's class?" Tony asked in a concerned voice as he and Mike were walking to school on Friday morning.

"I hope so," Mike replied.

The following Monday morning Tony picked up the same conversation. "We've got to win this challenge match," he announced forcefully. "Do you think Sammy can really pull it off?"

"He's got as good a chance as any of the rest of us," Mike assured him.

By Tuesday Tony had decided that they had to help. "Let's ask Sammy if he needs some sugge—"

"Stop worrying," Mike interrupted.

"Trust him. Besides, it's against the rules. If we know ahead of time what his mystery is about, then we can't try to answer it ourselves if Mr. Carlysle's class gets stumped."

The following afternoon, however, when the slender, dark-haired boy moved to the front of the crowded library to present his mystery, Mike wished Sammy looked more confident. As he squeezed his way between the rows of seats, his usually graceful body looked tight and awkward, and his lips were drawn into a pale, thin line.

Sammy cleared his throat, rubbed a nervous hand along his chin, then began to speak in a low voice. "My story took place quite a long time ago."

"Louder!" Butch Ogrodnick called from a spot in the centre of the third row. "Unless that's your brilliant plan for beating us— talking so softly we can't hear the clues."

Again Sammy brushed a hand across his chin then, in a slightly louder voice, repeated, "My mystery took place a long time ago." He paused for a moment and swallowed nervously before continuing, "Once—"

"Oh, no!" Butch Ogrodnick interrupted in a loud whisper deliberately pitched to carry all over the room. "He's gonna say 'Once upon a time,' and I'm gonna be sick! Come on, Tim. Let's get out of here."

By this time Sammy was so flustered that the hand holding his notes was shaking visibly. Quickly he put the paper down and tucked both hands out of sight behind his back. "My story was told to me by my grandfather," he hurried on, trying to ignore the interruptions. He was no longer looking at anyone, and his head was bowed defensively over his notes. "It's about a tribe of Blackfoot Indians, and it takes place in the days when the Blackfoot still hunted buffalo for their livelihood."

Butch Ogrodnick groaned loudly, then added, "If this is the alternative, I think I'd rather have had 'once upon a time.' "

It was more than Windy Jackson could take. He was sitting on the floor at the end of the front row next to Mike. Now, his face white with anger, he started scrambling to his feet.

"Sit still," Mike whispered, grabbing his arm.

Windy continued scrambling. "No way. Ogrodnick is out to make mincemeat of Sammy. I'll read his mystery. Butch won't dare try to hassle me that way."

Mike's grip tightened on Windy's arm. "Sammy's got to do it alone," he insisted in the same quiet whisper, "and you've got to let him. Otherwise he'll have Butch on his back for the rest of his life."

"He can't do it alone," Windy whispered back, still struggling to break free. "Butch has got him too upset."

It was true. From the start Sammy had looked terrified. Speaking to a whole roomful of people, some of whom he hardly even knew, was an ordeal he'd had to steel himself to face. Even if everything had gone well, it would have been tough for him. But Butch's interruptions had completely shattered his self-confidence.

"In another minute he won't be able to talk at all," Windy continued anxiously. "Somebody else has got to read his story for him. Lemme go."

"Give him a minute." Mike's voice was sure and steady but his heart was sinking. Sammy's silence was stretching out too long. It was twenty seconds now, maybe longer, that he'd been standing motionless, head bowed over his notes, his knuckles white as he gripped the edges of the lectern. Mike concentrated furiously on the slender figure at the front of the room, willing him to stand up to Butch Ogrodnick—urging him—

Sammy remained silent.

Reluctantly, Mike released his grip on Windy's arm.

But as Windy was getting to his feet, Sammy's head lifted. His face was still white and a muscle at the edge of his jaw was pulsing noticeably, but his shoulders had straightened. Looking right at Butch Ogrodnick, he said in a firm, clear voice, "No one has to stay who doesn't want to. But it's my story, and I'm going to tell it my way."

"Good for you," a blonde-haired girl from Mr. Carlysle's class applauded. She turned and glared at Butch. "Maybe you don't want to hear Sammy's story, but the rest of us do, so either be quiet or leave. Okay?"

It was all Mike could do not to cheer.

"As I said," Sammy continued, "this is a story my grandfather told me about a tribe of Blackfoot Indians who lived in the foothill country of Southern Alberta in the days before the Canadian Pacific Railroad was completed.

"The Tribe's most prized possession was a symbolic buffalo stone that was kept in a leather pouch. It had been handed down from one generation of elders to the next, and was kept in a special place in the chief's tipi."

"A stone buffalo, I could imagine, but what's a buffalo stone?" Sven Olafsen asked.

A chorus of 'shhhh's' came from the club members. They had agreed ahead of time not to ask any questions or help the other class in any way with the answer.

"Sorry," mumbled Sven to no one in particular. "I forgot."

But for the first time since Sammy's ordeal had started, he was smiling. "Sven's question's not giving anything away," he told the club members. Then to the rest of the room he went on. "Buffalo stones are small fossils that are shaped like buffalo. The Indians considered them to be one of the most powerful of all the spirit talismans. Since the buffalo itself provided them with everything they needed to stay alive—food, hide for clothing and shelter, bone for tools—they believed that the buffalo stone would give them advice when they needed it."

"How?" Sven asked again.

"By pointing," Sammy replied. "The only time the buffalo stone was taken out of its buffalo skin pouch was when the tribal elders wanted to know where game could be found or how to avoid an enemy ambush. Then with great solemnity the small fossil would be taken out of its pouch and thrown. Whatever direction it pointed in when it landed was the way the tribe was to go."

Sammy paused and scanned his notes for a

moment before continuing. "Among the members of this Blackfoot tribe was a twelve-year-old boy named Skylark."

A loud guffaw came from Butch's direction. "Nobody's got a name like that!"

Immediately the blonde girl from Mr. Carlysle's room pushed her chair back with a squeak and prepared to get to her feet in Sammy's defence. But Sammy didn't need rescuing.

He was looking straight at Butch Ogrodnick, and before the girl or anyone else could speak, he said evenly, "I guess you don't know much about Native culture. Symbolic names were used all the time, especially when people were young. Usually they were in the tribe's own tongue, but since my grandfather told me the story in English, he translated the names into English too."

For the first time Butch's self-satisfied smirk faltered. Sinking deeper into his chair, he gave a half-embarrassed glance first one way and then the other, as if checking to see if anyone was laughing at him.

Mike exchanged a grin with Tony and let out the breath he'd been holding in a long sigh. He settled back to enjoy the rest of the meeting.

"Unfortunately Skylark is a disappointment to his father," Sammy went on. "When all the other boys in the village are out racing their ponies over dangerous winding trails, or diving into the icy water to try to catch fish, Skylark prefers to be off by himself in the forest making friends with the animals. The squirrels will sit on his shoulder when he calls them, and even the deer make no move to run when he comes among them.

"The chief's son, Little Raven, thinks Skylark is a sissy. Not only that, he tells everyone that Skylark is letting the rest of the tribe down by not training himself to be a great hunter.

"Of course there are lots of other ways a person can be of use to his people besides being a great hunter. Skylark tries to point that out, but no one listens.

"Before long Little Raven has everyone in the village believing that Skylark is a coward —everyone except Skylark's father. He still has faith in his son. He tells Little Raven and the rest of the villagers that Skylark will prove that he is not a coward and not a disgrace to his people by joining in the big hunt that is planned to start the very next week. This last hunt of the summer is long and often dangerous, for it must provide sufficient food to keep the tribe all through the winter.

"Skylark would just as soon not go,

because he doesn't like killing. But he realizes that the hunt is necessary if his people are to live through the months of cold weather, so he agrees.''

Sammy paused for a moment to check the rows of listeners. Every face was looking back at him with interest—even Butch Ogrodnick's.

''A few days before the big hunt is scheduled to begin, a group of travellers stumble into the Blackfoot village. They have been on a hunting trip, but their knowledge of nature is so poor that for the past two weeks they have been wandering aimlessly through the woods, hopelessly lost. At this point they are half-starved and ill with fever.

''The Blackfoot take them in. They feed them and doctor them, and as they recover, encourage them to share in all the activities of the village.

''Before long the visitors learn of the existence of the buffalo stone. They beg to be allowed to see it, but the chief refuses. He explains that it is a valuable spirit symbol and must remain safely stored away in his tipi, except for those special occasions when its help is needed.''

Again Sammy consulted his notes. ''The arrival of the visitors causes the Blackfoot to postpone their hunting party. Now, however, the visitors seem well enough to travel. Accordingly it is decided that on the following morning everyone will leave the camp together. The visitors will continue on their way, and the Blackfoot hunters will start off on their delayed hunting trip. To celebrate their final evening together, the Blackfoot stage a big farewell party.

"It is a great party and everyone has a terrific time. But after a while Skylark slips away. He wants one final evening alone in the forest with his animal friends. Leaving the others around the campfire, he heads toward a high mossy cliff that overlooks the whole area. It is a favourite spot of his because from there he can see in all directions.

"But before he reaches the cliff, he realizes that there are other people on the trail. Two of the guests have also left the campfire.

"Skylark is just about to move away from them when their voices carry back to him on the evening air. They are making plans for tomorrow—plans to leave the camp as expected in the morning but to sneak back after they separate from the Blackfoot and steal the buffalo stone.

"Skylark can't believe it! People don't steal from their friends! Not when those friends have given them hospitality for over a week! Besides, don't the visitors realize that a spirit symbol is of no value to anyone but its rightful owner?

"He knows he must tell the elders what he has heard, so he hurries back to the campfire. But before he can finish explaining, Little Raven steps forward from the shadows where he has been listening. He says that Skylark's story is ridiculous. There is no way the visitors would plan to steal the buffalo stone for it would be of no use to them, and he accuses Skylark of making the story up so that he won't have to go on the hunt.

"The elders are very angry. They say that unless Skylark admits his story is a lie, he will no longer be considered a member of the tribe.

"Skylark is shattered for it is a terrible punishment, but he refuses to back down. He urges the elders to believe him and to do something to protect the buffalo stone.

"For a moment it seems that no one is going to listen, then a senior elder speaks up. Perhaps Skylark is telling the truth after all, he says. To find out, he suggests that in the morning, when the others set out on their hunt, Skylark should remain behind. If his story is true and the visitors really do return to steal the buffalo stone, it will be up to him to stop them. By so doing he will be able to prove not only his bravery, but also his loyalty to the tribe.

" 'He is only a boy!' another elder protests. 'What can a boy do against four grown men?'

" 'If he wishes to prove himself he must think of something,' the senior elder replies.

"All night long Skylark lies awake trying to do just that, but when morning arrives he still hasn't managed to come up with an idea."

Sammy paused a moment to catch his breath. As he had been telling his story all trace of his nervousness had disappeared.

"Early in the morning the visitors leave, accompanied by the Blackfoot hunting party. Actually the hunting grounds are in a different direction, but the Indians are anxious to make sure their new friends find their way safely, so they plan to take them to where there is a clearly marked path to follow. Then when they know their guests are headed in the right direction, they will say goodbye and circle back to the hunting grounds.

"Shortly after sun-up both groups are ready to leave. For a while after they have gone Skylark is busy with chores. Then he heads for his mossy cliff.

"From the cliff top he can see the cross-roads in the distance. He can see the Blackfoot hunters and their guests moving toward it. When they reach the fork, there is a moment of leave-taking. Then the visitors start along the left-hand fork, which will lead them back to the fort they came from, while the Blackfoot take the right one, which will bring them around in a large circle in the direction of the hunting grounds.

"Skylark continues to watch, and for a moment he feels a surge of hope, because the visitors are continuing along the left-hand fork. Maybe they've changed their minds and aren't coming back to steal the buffalo stone after all. But his hopes are short-lived. As soon as the Blackfoot are out of sight, the travellers stop and turn around. As Skylark's stomach tightens into a cold hard knot, they start sneaking back the way they have come.

"By this time Skylark is trembling all over. The second elder was right, he realizes. How can a twelve-year-old boy outsmart four grown men? However, he has to try. Somehow he must think of a plan that will not only save the buffalo stone but will do so in such a way that the elders realize he was not lying about the danger.

"Taking three deep breaths to stop himself from shaking, Skylark forces himself to think.

"Slowly an idea starts forming in the back

of his mind. He studies the landscape
stretched out before him. He locates the spot
he is looking for. He checks the position of
the sun in the sky. The hunting party and the
visitors left the village shortly after daybreak.
It is now past midmorning. That means it will
be afternoon before the visitors manage to
make their way back again, since they must
now move less openly. With a final glance at
the sun, Skylark scrambles down from the
cliff and hurries back to the village.

"His pony is grazing in the field behind the
tipis. He puts a rope bridle on it, leads it to a
clump of trees where it will be out of sight
and leaves it tied there. Then he slips into the
chief's tipi and gets the buffalo stone from its
secret hiding place. Holding it carefully, he
hurries out of the campsite to the place he
selected from the cliff top—a wide-open
clearing where a tall tree stands all alone.

"The rays of the morning sun are warm
and strong, and as they hit the single tall tree
in the clearing, they cast a long shadow onto
the open ground on the other side. Skylark
smiles with satisfaction. Picking up the
shovel he has brought with him, he walks
along the length of the shadow. When he
reaches its very tip he stops and begins to dig.

"When he is satisfied that he has dug deep
enough, he puts the buffalo stone safely

wrapped in its leather pouch into the hole. He covers it over, smooths the ground until it is impossible to see that it has been disturbed, and returns to the village.

"Finding a bit of smooth birchbark and a sharp piece of stone, Skylark makes a map. It is a sketch of the clearing showing the tall tree and the bright sun, and the tree's shadow on the ground. At the tip of the shadow he scratches an X, and a small symbol: Then he puts the bit of birchbark in the pocket of his trousers and sits down to wait."

Sammy paused for a moment.

"As Skylark estimated, it is early afternoon by the time the visitors make their way back to the village. Knowing all the men are off hunting, they head directly for the chief's tipi where they know the buffalo stone is kept. When they discover that it is gone they are furious. They seize Skylark. 'Where is the buffalo stone?' they shout.

" 'Why do you want it?' Skylark protests. 'It is no good to you.'

"The men refuse to listen. They begin to shake Skylark, demanding again that he tell where the stone is.

" 'Safe,' Skylark manages to stammer. 'You'll never find it.' As he speaks he clamps one hand over his pocket as though to protect something.

" 'He's hiding something!' one of the robbers shouts. He grabs Skylark and searches his pocket. 'Look!' and he holds up the map.

"As he does so his grip on Skylark loosens. Skylark breaks free and races for the trees behind the campsite where his pony is tied.

"One of the men starts after him but the others call him back. 'Let him go,' they say. 'We've got what we wanted.' He points to the clearly marked X on Skylark's map. Without another glance in Skylark's direction all four of them start looking for the place that matches the scene on the piece of birchbark.

"It takes them a while, but eventually they find the only place in the area where one tall tree stands alone in a clearing. They hurry to the tip of the tree's shadow and start to dig.

"Skylark, meanwhile, has galloped off to intercept the hunting party. By this time they have been travelling for half a day, but in a semi-circle. Their position, therefore, in a direct line with the village, is only several kilometres north.

"Skylark knows the country thoroughly from his many visits with his animal friends. He uses every available short-cut, and within a very short time succeeds in intercepting the others. He tells them what has happened.

"Immediately the chief, Skylark's father,

Little Raven and three braves leave the rest of the hunters and follow Skylark back to the village. When they reach the clearing, Skylark advances alone.

"The robbers are still digging. By this time they have dug a trench four metres in length without finding any sign of the buffalo stone. It is obvious that they are hot and tired and angry.

" 'Where is it?' they shout the moment they see Skylark. 'This map is a trick!' Throwing it on the ground, they move to seize Skylark.

"The chief, Skylark's dad, Little Raven and the other three braves now come forward.

"Skylark's father picks up the map. 'When did you draw this?' he asks his son.

" 'Early this morning,' Skylark replies. 'As soon as I saw from the cliff top that the visitors were coming back.'

"Skylark's father nods slowly. A smile flickers at the corner of his lips, but there is no other sign of emotion in his face. He hands the map to the chief. For a moment the chief, too, seems in danger of smiling. He hands the map to Little Raven, then turns to the robbers. He tells them how disappointed he is that they would repay Blackfoot kindness in such a way. He says they deserve to be punished, but that having to admit they have been outsmarted by a twelve-year-old boy should be punishment enough. He orders them out of the village and tells them never to come near the Blackfoot people again.

"Then to Little Raven he says quietly, 'I think you owe Skylark an apology. He is not a coward. In fact,' and he looks straight at Skylark as he says this, 'he is a credit to his people.' "

Sammy stopped talking. He looked around the silent library. "That's my story. How did Skylark outwit the robbers, and where was the buffalo stone?"

Mike held his breath. He glanced sideways at Tony. From the look of things Tony was holding his breath too.

For a long moment the only thing that broke the silence was a shuffling of feet, then someone said hesitantly, "Maybe Skylark only pretended to bury the buffalo stone. Maybe he had it in his pocket all the time."

Sammy shook his head. "The robbers would have found it when they searched him looking for the map."

"Maybe they didn't dig deep enough. Maybe it was down farther," someone else suggested.

Sammy shook his head again.

"I guess we give up," the blonde-haired girl said at last.

A chorus of cheers came from the members of the Mystery Club, but Sammy called for quiet. "Do the club members give up too?"

"No way," Mike answered happily. And he proceeded to give the answer.

What was Mike's solution? *Turn to page 156 and see if you are right.*

The Secret of Smugglers' Cove

For the next two days the members of the Mystery Club were riding high. They could talk of nothing but the chores they were going to assign to their "slaves" during the week to come. But on Friday Mike plummeted back to earth when he met Mr. Tate in the corridor.

"All set for Parents' Night?" Mr. Tate asked cheerily.

Mike felt as if a huge hole had just opened up beneath his feet.

"What are we going to do?" he asked Tony as they were leaving school that afternoon. "We've been so busy worrying about the challenge match that we've forgotten all about the Parents' Night presentation. It's next Friday and we've got nothing ready."

"I just wish we could repeat Sammy's mystery."

"So do I, but we can't. So for once in your

125

life be helpful and suggest something.''

"Okay, I will." Tony sounded defensive.

Mike waited expectantly.

''My suggestion,'' Tony began at last with the air of one deep in thought, ''is . . .'' He paused, then finished in an altogether different tone, ''that we ask Laura and Kathy.'' He nodded toward the two girls deep in conversation a short distance ahead.

Mike couldn't help grinning.

''Do you think it's possible,'' Laura said after the boys had caught up with them and Mike had repeated his question, ''that belonging to a Mystery Club can give people ESP? The mystery for Parents' Night is exactly what we were talking about!''

Tony nodded his head solemnly. ''I saw a program about that on TV. They said membership in any kind of club could do that to you, but particularly in one where mental activity was needed.''

Kathy and Laura were listening wide-eyed.

But the round-eyed looks gave way to pained grins as Laura and Kathy realized Tony was kidding.

Mike had taken a step backward out of Tony's line of vision. Now casting a secretive sideways glance at his friend, he whispered, ''Ignore him.'' He was shielding the words with the back of his hand. ''His mom dropped him on his head when he was little, but nobody talks about it.''

Tony's arm shot sideways but Mike was too quick. He ducked nimbly and let the arm whiz past his ear. Then in a casual tone, as if the earlier conversation had never been interrupted, he remarked, ''If you were thinking the same thing, what did you come up with?''

''That it should be a group project,'' Laura replied.

''You mean everybody write it?''

''One person write it, but everybody tell it.''

A frown came across Mike's face. ''Act it out, you mean?''

''Not exactly . . . . More a question of talk it out.''

With exaggerated enthusiasm Mike wiped his brow. ''Whew! I thought for a minute you meant we really had to act. If you had I'm afraid I'd be voting with Butch on the issue of cruelty to captive parents.''

Laura gave him the same look she'd given Tony a moment before, then continued, ''One person could be narrator and fill in the description and background details, and other people could take the parts of the people in the story.''

''Hey! A neat idea,'' Tony exclaimed. A

gleam had come into his brown eyes. "If we're all involved in doing the presentation, obviously we can't solve the mystery, which means it's going to be up to the parents."

"Except that the rest of the school is going to be there too," Laura reminded him.

The excitement drained from Tony's freckled face. "Another dream shattered," he muttered dramatically. "Think of the great loss of image there'd have been if the parents hadn't been able to come up with an answer. It could have advanced the whole question of kids' power to where we were totally in the driver's seat."

The other three burst out laughing at the picture Tony's words conjured up.

"That still doesn't solve the problem of what we're going to use for a mystery," Mike said when the laughter had subsided. "Come on, people, think."

But Laura and Kathy had done all the thinking they intended to do. With an airy wave of her hand, Laura took Kathy's arm and started moving in the other direction. "That's your department. Ours was suggesting the way to present it, and we've done that. Besides, we haven't got time. We've got to listen to a couple of new Bryan Adams tapes that Kathy just bought." And leaving the boys staring after them, they set off across the schoolyard in the direction of Kathy's house.

"Great," Tony grumbled. "Where are we gonna get an idea?"

"Let's try the library." Mike started back toward the school and Tony fell into step beside him.

Half an hour later they'd found what they needed.

A record crowd turned up the following Friday evening for Parents' Night. The Mystery Club presentation was scheduled as the final item on the program.

"To give everyone a chance to skip out before it starts," Butch Ogrodnick remarked dryly as the club members pushed past him on their way to the stage.

"Then why aren't you leaving?" Windy retorted. "If you stay you could be the only person in the auditorium who can't come up with the answer."

Butch's face flushed scarlet, but before he could reply Windy was six rows away.

Mike was first up onto the stage, positioning himself at the lectern which had been set up at the left. The rest of the club members took their places backstage. Briefly Mike explained how the Mystery Club worked. "We're counting on someone in the audience to solve the mystery," he finished.

A murmur of surprised comment greeted that statement and there was an exchange of amused looks.

"Our mystery takes place on the west coast of Vancouver Island," Mike began. "Somehow streams of electronic devices such as TVs, tape recorders, stereos, VCRs and computers are coming into British Columbia from the United States and Japan without any duty being paid on them, and the police are baffled.

"The goods aren't coming in by any of the usual routes because security measures have been tightened everywhere. The airport and the railway stations are all under close surveillance. All border crossing points are being watched, roadblocks have been set up on all the highways, guards have even been stationed at strategic places along the coastline. The only thing the police find suspicious is the movement of some of the fishing boats offshore."

Sven Olafsen and Kathy Chiu stepped forward from where they'd been standing with the others at the back of the stage. A murmur of appreciation came from the audience, because Sven was dressed in the uniform of a senior Customs official, the stiff brim of his hat sitting low on his forehead. Kathy wore the uniform of the

Royal Canadian Mounted Police.

"It has to be those fishing boats that are bringing in the contraband goods," Sven announced in a loud gruff voice.

Kathy was not convinced. "There are always fleets of small fishing boats in the waters off the west coast," she protested, "but there's nothing illegal about what they do. They simply head out early in the morning, before sunrise sometimes, and fish till dark. Then, when they've made their catch, they come into port and unload it at the fish docks."

"Exactly. But that's not what some of those small boats are doing," Sven insisted. "Look out there." He peered into space over the heads of the audience as if he was looking at the fishing fleet. "What do you see?"

"Not much because it's getting dark," Kathy admitted, raising a pair of binoculars to her eyes and looking in the same direction. "But I can see some of the boats starting to come in with their catch."

"Describe what they're doing."

"What do you mean, describe what they're doing?" Kathy sounded like a long-suffering mother plagued by questions from a three-year-old. "They're sailing into the fishing docks and unloading their fish."

"All of them?"

"As many as I can— No! Wait a minute! There's one that isn't. And there's another. In fact there are four that aren't. They started to come in, but for some reason they've stopped about two kilometres offshore." She was continuing to peer through the binoculars. "Now they're dropping anchor."

"Doesn't that strike you as strange?" Sven asked in a self-satisfied tone.

Kathy was still watching through the binoculars. "It does if they have fish on board," she agreed. "If they anchor out there and don't dump their catch till tomorrow morning the fish will spoil."

Sven nodded smugly.

"You mean they will stay out there all night?"

"Or somewhere nearby. We can't tell exactly because there's lots of movement within the fishing fleet once it's dark, and it's impossible to tell one boat from another. Some boats decide to head back out to sea to get an early start on the next day's fishing, others jockey for a better berthing position, and some just get restless and decide to cruise up and down the coast for a while."

Kathy was silent for a moment, still studying the fishing fleet through her binoculars. "There's still no reason to suspect them of smuggling," she said at last. "Perhaps they're anchoring way out there instead of coming in to shore because they haven't caught any fish."

"Except they have," Sven countered. "They've caught lots of fish. Maybe not a full load, but at least half of one. Tomorrow morning around 6 or 7 A.M. they'll come in to the fish docks and unload barrels of rotting fish that would have earned them four times as much money if they'd unloaded them ten hours earlier."

Kathy stared at him in amazement. "Is that what they're doing?"

Sven nodded.

"Often?"

"A couple of times this week, three times last week, and at least once the week before."

"The same boats?"

Again Sven nodded.

The spotlight that had been focussed on the Customs Officer and the Mountie dimmed and moved to Mike at the lectern.

"The more the authorities thought about these fishing boats," he said taking over the story, "the more puzzling it seemed. They were convinced that somehow these boats must be involved in the smuggling operation, but the question was how? At last they decided to call on the Coast Guard and the

Army for assistance.''

Windy, wearing a Coast Guard uniform, and Laura, Sammy and Whiz in Canadian Army fatigues moved to centre stage.

"The Coast Guard will keep the fishing boats under surveillance every day till it gets dark,'' Windy announced. "Then it's your turn,'' he told soldiers Laura, Sammy and Whiz. "You've got to post guards along the coastline. I want them at hundred-metre intervals wherever it would be possible for anyone to land. Is that clear, Sergeant?''

Sammy saluted smartly. "Yes, sir! We'll put a guard every hundred metres from the southern tip of the Island right up to the northern tip. Not even a duck will be able to land without someone noticing.''

Windy grinned. "Don't overdo it, soldier. Put a guard every hundred metres in all the areas where a boat could land, but don't waste men in the spots where they aren't needed.''

"Sir?'' Sammy asked politely.

"Have a good look along this coastline. There are lots of places where there's no beach or shallow water to land a boat in. The ocean water comes bang up against a sheer two-hundred-metre-high cliff. There's no point in posting guards in places where no one could possibly manage to come ashore.''

Sammy shuffled his heavy army boots. "Yes, sir," he agreed in a subdued tone. Then shouting to his company to follow, he marched briskly around the stage. At the far corner he positioned Whiz as the first lookout. A dozen paces away he positioned Laura as the second, then took up the third position himself the same distance further along.

The spotlight returned to Mike. "It was hoped that this surveillance would stop the flow of contraband goods into the province, but the numbers of illegal TVs, stereos, computers, radios and VCR's on B.C.'s black market increased every day.

"The Customs Officer decided to ask for more help. Convinced that there must be an obvious answer to how the smuggled goods were being landed, he sent word to the University of British Columbia and to the University of Victoria, asking if their best authorities would offer advice.

"The first to answer was the University of Victoria Geography Department, who sent their senior geographer."

A figure wearing a black academic gown and mortarboard moved with heavy steps to centre stage. It was Maribel Turvey. Turning to Customs Officer Sven and Mountie Kathy who had returned to centre stage with her, Maribel said with formality, "To solve a case of this sort one must keep in mind the physical characteristics of the terrain. Certain conditions lend themselves to smuggling, and it is in the areas where these conditions are present that you should be centring your search.''

''What sort of conditions?'' Sven asked.

''Two things primarily—inlets and caves. Either can provide smugglers with just the secret avenue they need. It is not too difficult for an enterprising band of smugglers who have discovered a cave situated at sea level to link that cave by tunnel to an escape outlet some distance away. With the constant rise and fall in water level caused by the incoming and outgoing tides the cave is not even visible much of the time. As a result it often escapes the notice of the authorities.''

Sven and Kathy nodded thoughtfully.

''Even more useful to smugglers are the inlets,'' Maribel went on. ''There are dozens of these up and down the coastline, and they too often escape the notice of the authorities. At low tide they only extend a short distance inland, but at high tide they turn into tiny water highways leading many kilometres into the countryside. The fact that their banks are often lush with undergrowth makes them even more attractive to the smugglers, because the greenery provides camouflage. A carefully packed barge moving silently down one of these high-tide highways has an excellent chance of escaping notice.''

Sven thanked the Geography professor. He waited till she had gone, then called excitedly, ''Where is the Coast Guard Captain?'' When Windy emerged from the shadows at the back of the stage, Sven ordered, ''Summon your officers! At high tide tomorrow check the entire area for caves and inlets!''

''Does it have to be just at high tide?'' Windy asked.

''Of course it has to be at high tide! Weren't you listening to the Geography professor? It's only at high tide that smugglers will be using the inlets. That is the only time they flow far enough inland to be useful. That is probably the reason you have noticed those fishing boats cruising along the coast in the evening. They're waiting for high tide. Assemble your men. At high tide tomorrow begin your search.''

''Right,'' Windy replied. And he marched off obediently. Sven rubbed his hands together in satisfaction as he watched him go. ''Well, Constable,'' he said to Kathy who was standing beside him. ''Looks like we've got this case just about wrapped up.''

Again the spotlight moved from Sven and Kathy to the lectern at the side of the stage.

"As the Coast Guard Captain headed off to follow the Custom Officer's orders," Mike said, taking up the story, "a History professor from the University of British Columbia arrived."

Tony stepped forward this time, also wearing an academic cap and gown. "I heard what my learned friend just said. She is quite right in urging you to consider the physical condition of the area, but you must also remember that history has a tendency to repeat itself. The answer to your current problem may be found by studying similar cases from the past. Today's smugglers may be imitating a scheme invented by some earlier group."

The assurance that had marked Sven's expression a moment earlier, drained away. "What sort of scheme?" he asked, no longer quite so sure that the case was solved.

"Perhaps something like the sunken houseboat scheme that was used in Lake Michigan during Prohibition," Tony replied. "A group of enterprising Canadian smugglers sank a houseboat off the American shoreline and hooked up an underwater rope pulley system from the boat to a house on the American beach. They stored their home-made liquor on it till they were sure no patrols were watching, then they sent it to shore by means of the rope pulley system.''

For the second time Sven's face lit with excitement. ''Maybe the smugglers aren't using caves or inlets after all,'' he exclaimed to Kathy. ''Maybe they're using an underwater pulley! Maybe they're anchoring offshore because that's where their sunken barge is. Maybe as soon as it's dark they're unloading the smuggled goods and storing them in some sort of watertight barrels on the barge. Then during the night when no one can see, they're sending the barrels and their smuggled goods in to shore on a pulley system, just the way the professor described!''

Kathy was just as excited as Sven. ''That would explain why they don't bring their fish in till morning,'' she agreed. ''They can't. If they try to dump their fish while they've still got smuggled goods on board, someone is bound to notice. And that also explains the half cargo. How can they carry a full load of fish when the boats are already half-filled with computers and TVs and stereos.''

Sven was beaming. ''Shall I tell our Customs people to follow up on this and arrest the crews of the fishboats, or do the Mounties want to do it?''

''First we'd better catch them in the act,'' Kathy replied. With a brisk salute, she headed off stage in the same direction Windy had taken.

"But," Mike continued from the lectern, "four days later the Mountie and the Coast Guard Captain returned. The Mountie reported that a thorough search of the entire area by trained divers had revealed no sunken boats, pulley lines or cables leading from the water to any house or shed or boathouse on shore.

"The Coast Guard Captain reported a similar lack of success. On four consecutive nights when the tide was at its highest, they checked the entire coastline. No caves of any kind could be found. And though there were lots of inlets as the geographer had suggested, no goods were being smuggled ashore by that route. Each night the Coast Guard posted observers along each one of them. Nothing was being brought into the country that way. Yet the flow of smuggled goods was continuing at an even greater rate than before."

Mike looked up from his notes and studied the faces in the audience. "That's our mystery. The airports and railway stations were being watched, there were roadblocks on the highways, all the border crossing points were being watched. The only way the goods could possibly be coming in was by water. Obviously the fishing boats were involved. But how? Guards had been set to watch all the inlets and the smugglers weren't using that route. The cliffs had been thoroughly searched at high tide four nights in a row and no caves of any kind had been discovered. And there were no underwater pulley systems. Somehow the goods were getting ashore, but how? Where could the authorities be going wrong?"

For a moment complete silence settled over the auditorium. Mike exchanged a quick look with Tony. It really would be something if the parents were stumped, he mused.

But before any of the parents had a chance to answer, Colin Turgenev, a grade five student from Mrs. Grimsby's class held up his hand, "I know," he said.

The applause was deafening when he finished explaining. While it was still echoing, the president of the Parents' Association got to her feet. "On the strength of that terrific applause I think we should ask for another Mystery Club presentation at the next Parents' Night."

Another round of applause greeted that remark.

A few moments later as the crowd filed from the auditorium Mike and Tony caught up with Colin.

"That was pretty good," Tony commended him, his voice warm with admiration. "It was probably one of the toughest mysteries we've had. Why haven't you joined the Mystery Club?''

A shy smile came over Colin's face. "I didn't know it was coming apart," he answered.

Mike doubled up with laughter. "At last here's someone who can give you your own back," he told Tony when he could speak. He turned to Colin. "You've got to join. We need you. Okay?''

"Okay," Colin agreed with a grin.

What was Colin's answer? *Turn to page 158 and see if you are right.*

SOLUTIONS

Solution #1—
Field Trip Folly

Tony's story was unlikely to be true because Spooky was a lab retriever, and retrievers are water dogs. They are often specially trained to jump into lakes and ponds to retrieve ducks. Spooky would have been more likely to swim across the swollen river than to look for a long way around.

Laura's story was also untrue. Admittedly she could have made the flares as she claimed and mounted them on branches. But they would have brought no rescuers. In the thick fog, the light from the flares would not have carried any distance—certainly not to a ranger station situated fifteen kilometres away and at the very top of the mountain.

Mike's story therefore is the true one. He worked out which direction to walk in by looking for moss on the trees.

Mike knew that in a dense forest where little direct sunlight penetrates, moss may grow on all sides of the trees. That is why he looked for a spot where the trees were far enough apart to allow the sun to get between them. He then carefully examined those trees because he knew that moss needs moisture and will not grow on the sides that the sun strikes and dries out. Over the course of a day, the sun will strike every side of such trees but one—the north side.

This is a standard technique taught in wilderness survival courses in areas where there is limited humidity and lots of sunshine, and where it is not difficult to find wooded areas where the trees are not too densely packed together.

Solution #2—
Inventions for Sale

Manny realized that one of the stamps on the empty envelope—the stamp that didn't bear the post office cancellation mark —was worth $25 000.

The thieves had heard Manny calling the police. They knew they would never succeed in getting the cheque out of the park, so they devised an ingenious scheme. They decided to exchange it for a single, very expensive postage stamp.

They waited till Manny and the police were on the other side of the park, then returned to the stamp display. They found a rare stamp worth exactly $25 000, bought it, then attached it to an envelope that one of the men had in his pocket. They knew the money was safe, because as soon as they had eluded the police and were free, all they had to do was return to the stamp display or find a stamp shop, and sell the stamp for their $25 000.

It was the fact that the two stamps on the letter were different, and that only one had been cancelled by the post office that first drew Manny's attention to them. Then when he looked closely he realized that the second stamp was not a regular stamp at all, but an extremely rare and unusual one.

Solution #3—
Brain Teasers

The answer to Mr. Proctor's number puzzle is not 17 but 47. Dividing by 1/2 is the same thing as multiplying by two. Four times 5 equals 20; 20 divided by 1/2 equals 40; 40 plus 7 equals 47.

As to how many of Farmer Jagg's pigs can say they are different in colour from any others, the answer is none, because pigs cannot talk.

If you said the story about the English army officer had something wrong with it, you are correct. It cannot be true. If the man died without awakening, his wife couldn't have known what he was dreaming about and therefore had no reason to feel responsible for his death.

Solution #4—
Olympic Intrigue

Mary used the hockey scores as a code to send her message. The number of goals each team had scored indicated the letter of the team name that was to be used. The message was: TARGET STEIB—*T*oronto 1, Phil*a*delphia 5; Mont*r*eal 5, Cal*g*ary 4; *E*dmonton 1, Bos*t*on 4; then W*a*shington 3, De*t*roit 3; N*e*w York 2, Winn*i*peg 5; Que*b*ec 4, Vancouver 0.

A code of this kind is easy to arrange and can be used with things like weather reports and price lists as well as with game scores.

The method used by cryptanalysts to "crack" codes varies according to the code used. Score card codes such as the one above are easy.

The method used for solving a letter substitution code like the one Julius Caesar used is more complicated. It is called "running down." A word of the message is selected, for example, NKRV. Underneath it the cryptanalyst writes MJQR. These are the letters just before the code ones in the alphabet. Then he or she writes LIPT, the letters one more space back. The cryptanalyst continues to "run down" the letters in this way till a recognizable word appears. In this instance the cryptanalyst would move back six places, when HELP would appear.

The cryptanalyst solves a password code by watching for repeated letters. In every language certain letters turn up more frequently than others, and in English the most commonly used letter is E. The next most common letter is T, then A, O, N, R, I, S, G, and D, in that order. The cryptanalyst counts the number of times each letter turns up in the message, then using that frequency key as a guide, does some switching and changing until the password emerges.

Solution #5—
The Disappearing Ornaments

Jamie realized, just as Mike had, that the magpie had taken the ornaments and hidden them in the tree outside.

Magpies are well known for their fascination with shiny bright-coloured objects. It would have been easy for the magpie to carry the ornaments by the strings that were used to attach them to the branches of the Christmas tree. The two small presents would have been equally easy for the bird to carry. It could have held them by their ribbons.

Solution #6—
Four Minute Wonder

The details about the kerosene lantern in Dinnigan's story convinced the junior reporter that the story was not true.

Dinnigan claimed that the smoke in the cabin was so thick he could not see through it, and that he had to hold his breath the whole time he was inside. He also said that the only thing that enabled him to find the hidden cash box was the light from the kerosene lantern he had taken with him.

If the cabin had been so full of smoke that Dinnigan could neither see nor breathe, the kerosene lantern would not have continued to burn. Certainly it would not have continued to burn at its brightest. The light of a kerosene lantern is made by the burning of the kerosene on the wick, and this can only happen if sufficient oxygen is present to allow for combustion.

As the junior reporter pointed out, if Dinnigan had lied about this detail in the story, he had probably made up the story itself, particularly since the old prospector had never been seen by anyone else.

Solution #7—
Science Fair

As soon as the girl from Bennington heard where the Westbank water samples had come from, she knew that the rival school's water study project would not win the Science Fair.

The water lilies and minnows being used in the study had been taken, as Bennington's had, from nearby fresh water lakes. Therefore they could be used for growth study in the water samples from the Red River, Lake Ontario and Lake Superior. They could not, however, be used for growth study in the water samples from Georgia Strait, the Strait of Juan de Fuca or the Bay of Fundy. These are all bodies of salt water. Even Hudson Bay and the lower St. Lawrence River have a sufficiently high salt content to endanger the life of fresh water minnows.

Solution #8—
Balloon Race Mystery

Daphne knew from her training that the most likely reason for a balloon to have trouble gaining altitude is because it is carrying too much weight. It didn't seem possible, however, that the blue and green balloon could have any difficulty carrying a two-man crew when it had such an outsized air chamber. Once she was sure the inexperienced team had not forgotten to close the top valve, she knew that they must be carrying something exceptionally heavy—such as the ten gold bars.

That was what her father had meant when he had tried to reason with the police, she realized. He'd been trying to point out that if he'd been carrying 320 kilograms of gold he'd have found it difficult to climb very far off the ground, even with no other crew members on board. Certainly he wouldn't have been able to "shoot up into the sky" as the security guards had claimed.

Admittedly the blue and green balloon had been built with an outsized air chamber, for the robbers had realized that they would need extra lifting power if they expected to spirit the gold bricks away. But in their inexperience they did not realize the extent to which the rules of the race would limit them. Using the hot air rather than either helium or hydrogen, they would need an air chamber many times bigger again.

In 1783 Joseph Montgolfier experimented to see how large a hot air balloon would be needed to lift six men, whose weight totalled approximately 500 kilograms. He found his balloon had to be 42 metres high and 33 metres in diameter.

The robbers were carrying almost exactly the same weight with a two-man crew and ten gold bars. If they had been using either hydrogen or helium, both of which are much lighter than air, they would have been all right, but even though their hot air balloon was larger than any of the others, it was still much too small to carry that heavy a load.

Solution #9—
The Buffalo Stone

The buffalo stone was still hidden exactly where Skylark had buried it at mid-morning, at the tip of the shadow cast by the single tree. The robbers could not find it because they were digging at the tip of the shadow cast in mid-afternoon.

By the time the robbers got back to camp it was well past noon. By that time the sun was not in the same position it had been in when Skylark buried the stone. Not only had it climbed higher, it had also moved a considerable distance across the sky. As a result, the tree's shadow was considerably shorter and fell in a different direction.

Skylark knew he had to find a way to make the robbers show their hand if he was to prove to the chief and Little Raven that he hadn't been lying about the danger. That's why he came up with this scheme. Since the robbers knew so little about nature, they would almost certainly fail to consider how the movement of the sun would affect the tree's shadow. Skylark therefore gambled on the likelihood that they would keep digging unsuccessfully until he had time to bring the others back.

However, he also knew he had to make

sure that the buffalo stone was in no real danger, and that is why he put the symbol showing the position of the sun on his map. That way if something should happen to him, any member of the tribe could read the map and find the buffalo stone.

Skylark's Map

Solution #10—
The Secret of Smugglers' Cove

As the Coast Guard and the Mountie suspected, the smuggled goods were being brought into British Columbia by the fishing boats, but not by means of an underwater pulley system or along any of the inlets. They were being brought in through one of the many sea level caves that exist in the steep rock cliffs. The authorities did not discover these caves because they searched the shoreline only at high tide, when the sea level caves were all underwater.

The authorities were quite right to check the inlets at high tide, because that was when the inlets were most likely to be used. The caves, however, should have been searched for only at low tide.

A favourite trick of smugglers is to discover a large sea level cave along some isolated area of coastline, then dig a tunnel back from the cave to a secret opening in a hidden ditch or gulley. Ignoring the low tide that occurs in daylight hours, the smugglers wait for the low tide at night, then they simply sail along the coastline under cover of darkness till they reach their cave. There, accomplices are waiting to unload the smuggled goods and whisk them back through the tunnel to some secret hiding place.

They have to work quickly because in a short time the tide will start coming in again. Before long both the cave and the tunnel will be completely underwater. But this is the reason the method is so successful. During most of each twenty-four-hour cycle, except for a short time when the tide is at its lowest, the caves and the tunnels are completely invisible.

JOAN WEIR

Balloon Race Mystery is the second in the *Mystery Club* series and the thirteenth book Joan Weir has published. Of these, eight are novels for young people; the others are non-fiction books for adults. In addition, she has had a number of short stories published in national children's magazines, and three plays for children produced and toured by professional theatre companies.

Joan was born in Calgary and educated in Calgary and Winnipeg. At present she lives in Kamloops, British Columbia. She is an English instructor at Cariboo College in Kamloops and is an experienced teacher of creative writing. In private life, Joan is the wife of a Kamloops surgeon and the mother of four grown sons.